Ψ DEADLY RECKONING

*For John —
with best wishes
for good reading —
hope you find the world
of Psy Mind interesting.*

Ginny

VAL CHANDA

Val Chanda

Wasteland Press
www.wastelandpress.net
Shelbyville, KY USA

Psy Mind:
Deadly Reckoning (Book One)
by Val Chanda

First Printing – September 2011
ISBN: 978-1-60047-610-5

This is a work of fiction. Names, characters, places, and incidents either
are the product of the author's imagination or are used fictitiously, and
any resemblance to actual persons, living or dead, business
establishments, events, or locales is entirely coincidental.

Printed in the U.S.A.

0   1   2   3   4   5   6   7   8

To the other Val,
To Steve,
and
To anyone who has ever had a hunch.

Chapter One

Joleson Randle walked home alone down mean, ominous streets. His route took him through a decayed business district, row after row of old storefronts, shuttered and padlocked or boarded up. These streets offered little sense of security even by day. At night, they became a menacing pattern of light and shadow. Street lamps arcing overhead shed a relentless orange glow. Their bitter light revealed endless arabesques of spray paint that wandered over every available surface. But the light was always broken. It ended abruptly at alleys and entryways. They were dark blocks of shadow, blank but foreboding.

However, Joleson Randle walked confidently through the bleak pattern of orange and black. On the almost deserted streets were a few vagrants, a tired prostitute here or there, the footfalls of another walker somewhere behind him. They were all unworthy of his notice. As for anything the shadows might hold, Joleson Randle knew himself. His strength, his training, his discipline. He knew his skill with the knife he always carried. No one had ever even approached him. He believed his assurance encased him like armor. Still if he were ever mugged, he had no doubt what the outcome of that encounter would be.

So that night, as all the nights before, the grim orange and black streets which for most people were a place of necessity and fear were for Joleson Randle a place of solace, a place to be secure in the privacy of his own thoughts. The only place perhaps where he felt truly secure.

As was common for him, what dominated Joleson Randle's thoughts as he walked home that night was hatred. Hatred which had always come easily to him. He indulged in his hatred as a pastime both familiar and pleasurable. Of course, he did not call what he felt hatred. He called it reason and intelligence.

Tonight he had a specific focus for the hatred which consumed him. He liked that. He could hear in his mind the conversation in the bar earlier that evening. He could hear it, feel it, more clearly than he had ever recalled anything before.

It had been just the regular guys and Nick behind the bar. Things were maybe a little quieter than usual. Randle remembered bringing his hand down sharply. He could feel the sting of it hitting the bar as he said, "And I say the laws on them don't go anywheres near far enough. And if any of you had a fucking brain in your head, you'd say the same thing. At the meeting last week..."

"For chrisesake, you're always flappin' your yak about those damn meetings." That had been Carl, always the loudmouth.

Glancing from Carl to him, a couple of the guys had stirred restlessly. But he beat down his rage at the insult. One of them, Eddie it was, had said, "Come on, Jole, let's just have another beer and leave the problems of the world to them that has something to say about them."

He knew it was an attempt to quiet things down and his anger rose again. "That's the trouble with you people. The damn world goes to hell and you don't give a shit."

"Yeah, sure," Nick this time, with his meaningless bartender's agreement.

"Yeah, sure," he had echoed. "Is that what you're going to say?" He had turned to a couple of the other guys. "Is that what you're all going to say when they take over? They'll be running things, you know."

"So what," someone else had butted in. "The politicians run things, sometimes the crooks. Somebody always runs things. And all I know is it ain't me. And it's never gonna be me. Or you."

He had swung around and the man who had spoken took a step backwards. "You never lost your job because of one of them," he had said tightly. "I shoulda been a cop, you know."

"Yeah, so you said."

"Anyways, Jole, you can't be sure about that. It ain't even legal." Eddie again, always quieting, always smoothing things over.

"Legal," he had said scornfully. God, what assholes they were. To believe that made any difference.

Then he had slapped a printout from *The Free Thinker* website across the edge of the bar. "You oughta read some of this. That's what you oughta do. Here, listen to this. 'In years gone by, a nightmare vision was foretold wherein the forces of government would intrude on the inalienable privacy of the citizens by two way vids. We see today that vision proved false. In fact, interactive vids are one of the great benefits of modern life. But though the form of the vision was wrong, the nightmare still threatens. For what is the untrammeled presence of telepaths in our midst but the greatest invasion of privacy known in human history. They walk among us, they look like us, but without our knowledge and consent, they psych our inmost thoughts. A great fight looms before us. A fight for our most basic rights and liberties. The right of the majority to keep our thinking free from invasion by the freakish, and dangerous, psy perceiving minority.'"

"Sure, sure, Randle." The others had checked the time and finished up. "Meanwhile I gotta get home or the wife'll tell me something about freethinking."

Eddie had laughed, an irritating high pitched giggle. "Something about freethinking. That's a good one. Isn't that a good one, Jole?"

The rest of them had shuffled slowly out.

"Assholes," he had said.

Nick had leaned over and taken the printout from him. "What's 'untrammeled' mean?"

"Ah, you're all a bunch of assholes." With that he had stamped out.

And they were he thought. Up to guys like that nothing would happen. All they cared about was their paycheck, their booze, and fuck the wife regular, maybe a nightlady on the side once in a while.

But at least they were normal, even that son of a bitch Carl who had tried to shut him up. He should have taught him a lesson, but no, never lose sight of the real enemy. That's what Martin Bren always said. And he was right. Goddam fuckin' psikes. "We're sorry, J. Randle. The results of your personnel assessment indicate you would be more effective, and successful, in another line of work." That's what they'd said at his screening interview. "Personnel assessment." Shit. It had been a psike. Somebody in that group of shitass bureaucrats was a psike. Telling him he was no good. Just because they could tell how much he hated them.

"But it ain't even legal, Jole." He heard Eddie's words whining in his head again. How else could they have known so much about him? Not from their dumb ass tests. From a psike, that's how. You never knew where they were, what they took from you. Tell him the government didn't use that. Tell him that wasn't why he worked a crummy dead end job. I shoulda been a cop. Woulda been, except for them.

Someday, somebody's gonna do something. Someday, people are gonna wake up. Guy like Bren, he'd wake them up. People listened to him, a roomful, a crowd, it didn't matter. They listened. "The struggle is hard. We fight cowardice, complacency, and collusion. All the enemy's greatest weapons. The silent, relentless enemy, spreading among us, aided by the self-interest and moral decadence of our self-styled leaders.

"The task before us leaves no room for doubts, for hesitation. It must be our life. It is our life. If we know that, we will triumph, as human will and human spirit have always triumphed. Nothing can prevent us. Nothing, so long as we dedicate ourselves to the greatest work ever given to mankind. To save ourselves, justly to save ourselves, from the most dangerous enemy."

Yes, they listened to Martin Bren. Someday even jerks like the guys at the bar would listen. Someday. Soon. And Joleson Randle would be there, part of it, ready. Ready to do his part.

Joleson Randle's hatred vibrated within him. He could do whatever needed to be done. When it wasn't words anymore, then would be his time. He could feel it in himself, feel what it would be like. He would drive the knife in carefully. There would be no sliding off along hard resistant bone. There would be only the satisfying tension of muscle yielding to his strength. Then the sudden release as the knife, his knife, drove home to all the soft vulnerability beneath.

A shudder went through him. Each and every one, he could do it. If needed. "A great fight looms before us...The struggle is hard...To save ourselves from the most dangerous enemy." He was ready. The time was near. Then there would be safety again and limitless satisfaction. Maybe soon. Maybe.

Lost in the images within his mind, Joleson Randle automatically turned into the small alley which was a shortcut to the ramshackle apartment building where he lived. Somewhere at the far edge of his consciousness, he was barely aware that someone still walked behind him, but set against what he felt within himself, that presence from the outer world faded into insignificance.

He had often wandered through the images which now played in his mind, images in which he lived more fully than he lived anything else in his life. And tonight, they filled him as they never had before. He seemed to have found all of himself for the first time. The images in his mind had become reality, clear and complete. A reality of his own making, in a way he could not have imagined possible. A reality in which he, Joleson Randle, felt immeasurable power. The power of hatred fueling action. The power by which he, Joleson Randle, slashed through the alien presence, the psike menace which blind, stupid, normal people had allowed in their midst. He, Joleson Randle, would do for them what they could not do for themselves. He would deliver them. Murder after murder until the psikes were no more.

Without realizing it, Joleson Randle stopped walking. The footfalls behind him kept coming, but he no longer heard them. Unconsciously he put out an arm to steady himself against the side of the building. Exhausted, he panted, his head throbbed. Like an engine racing out of control, his mind played out its images. His knife rose and fell, rose and fell. But there were more and always more. The intensity of his hatred drove through his body. His heart beat fast and faster. It seemed his blood would burst through the walls of veins and arteries. Gasping, he fell to his knees, and then to the ground. He gave one last convulsive spasm and then his mind exploded within him. A final climactic merging of Joleson Randle and his hatred. After that his heart beat no longer.

In the quiet confines of an alley two doors from his apartment building, Joleson Randle died, burst apart by his own hatreds. His body, untouched by his assailant, lay crumpled in the shadows. Without stopping, the slow footfalls of the walker behind turned away and retreated into the night of orange light and black shadow.

Chapter Two

Jonas Acre drove up the long strip of old thruway which rose in a series of dips and rises into the mountains. The last mass transit facility was fifty miles behind him and he had another fifty miles to go. For the trip out to Tyler's, he had requisitioned one of the old manually operated vehicles still used by the Natural Preserve Service. He had been motivated partly by tact but also by the hope that the long solitary drive would give him additional time to prepare for the interview he faced at its end.

But that hope had proved illusory. Not even his seemingly undiminished skill in driving one of the old manuals dispelled the anxiety which seemed to settle more heavily upon him with each passing mile.

The country through which he traveled was beautiful. A land of old mountains, sprawling low, well battered by time, but still lushly tree covered. For long stretches, the road ran over the treetops, giving more a sensation of flight than of overland travel. The trees below, in full leaf, blotted out the ground. But their beauty, instead of soothing Jonas, seemed to amplify his disquiet. He knew that hidden beneath the solid green cover below were the remnants of small towns, now deserted. Towns which had been crumbling into ruin for the past thirty years. He would have liked to have seen a road, or a cleared plot of ground with a house, something to humanize this lovely, but implacable, landscape.

He told himself his reaction to the countryside was only a reflection of his discomfort with his errand. Maybe he should have asked Tyler to come in to Psy Management. He was pretty sure she would have complied and at least he would have been on his own turf, with maybe one less thing fueling his anxieties. But he had chosen what he knew was the more diplomatic way. A private visit to ask her to do what she would surely rather refuse, to get her to cooperate willingly rather than by force of law.

Besides he had to admit, much as it bothered him to do so, a good part of his mood could be traced directly to his anticipation of meeting with Tyler face to face. He liked her, trusted her, believed in her reliability. Their longstanding friendship went well beyond the demands of their official relationship. But despite all that and despite his years of association with them, he could never totally dispel a sense of unease around telepaths, especially high range psy perceivers, like Tyler. He knew his reaction was normal, but it seemed more fitting for some ignorant citizen who watched too many quikvids than for the Commissioner of the Department of Psyonic Management. He worried about it more than he should. His assistant Cal even kidded him about it. But it bothered him. It frustrated him too, knowing there was no way he could conceal his nervousness from Tyler.

Bad enough to come asking an unwelcome favor, worse to ask it while broadcasting anxiety about even having to deal with you. Still like most psy perceivers, Tyler seemed to take that response for granted. And if she'd ever been offended by the commonplace nervousness which even he could not suppress, she had never shown it. Unless her whole choice of environment revealed her true reaction. All high range telepaths preferred a fair amount of solitude, but Tyler seemed to need actual physical isolation. To get it, she had sought out this landscape which always made Jonas so acutely aware of its emptiness.

Tyler West lived on an unheard of thirty acres of privately owned land in the midst of what was now the natural preserve north of Philly Sector of NorEast Metro. The holding, originally far more extensive, had been in her family since before the turn of the century and this portion had somehow survived the Land Acquisition Act of the 20s. Jonas didn't know the details but keeping the land had undoubtedly been the work of Harry West who had been Tyler's grandfather and who had amassed the fortune which allowed her to maintain her very private, and eccentric, estate. It would have all made great copy for the gossip blogs and the quikvids if they could have tracked her down. Her house was of genuine stone. There was a garden, an orchard, animals. It all seemed to belong to another time.

But, in fact, the rusticity of Tyler's lifestyle was deceptive. She might use a good part of her considerable wealth to maintain her quaint environment, but there was also ample left over for the requirements of modern life. When Jonas had called to let her know he was coming, he had run into a new commsys, one that certainly had a later generation of technology than the one he used in his office at Psy Management. And that technology included the kind of security which insured Tyler would never become copy for the media, at least any more than her publishers could talk her into accepting. She wrote very popular detective novels marked by intricate plots and devastating characterization. Jonas had read them all. But as was the case with most writers, few of Tyler's readers would have recognized her if they had passed her on the street. Not that there was much chance of that, as infrequently as Tyler came into metro.

Still, country estate and all, Tyler certainly was not a crank. She conformed to all legal requirements, her psychological profiles were well within accepted parameters. Her writing gave her both personal and financial independence from her inherited wealth. In fact, she had as few quirks as any PsyCF4 he dealt with. Which was, after all, one of the reasons he had chosen her.

Jonas let the image of Tyler form in his mind. She had a pleasant but not particularly distinctive face. Nose, chin, average, neither prominent nor noteworthy. Short, medium brown hair, cut for convenience not style. She had gray eyes which at first glance also seemed unremarkable. Only if you looked closely, could you see the intelligence that lurked behind them. In fact, Jonas reflected, whenever he saw Tyler again after a long separation, his first thought was how ordinary she looked. His second was how deceptive that impression was. Naturally she always knew he had that reaction. It amused her.

In less time than he expected, Jonas found himself at the exit from the thruway which led to the back roads to Tyler's place. The thruway, despite the little use it got, was well maintained. It still provided an alternative to air transport as a means of accessing the natural preserves which stretched from Philly Sector all the way to Lake Ontario and the Canadian border. But once off its smooth pavement, Jonas had to proceed more slowly and more cautiously. Fortunately the entrance to Tyler's property was not far from the thruway exit. He logged in at the gate, drove past the house where the caretakers, a couple name Fuentes, lived. A few minutes later he arrived at Tyler's house.

When the rumble of the old manual vehicle finally stopped, Jonas was struck by the unaccustomed stillness. It took a few minutes before he sifted it into a variety of late afternoon sounds of birds and insects. Before he swung out of the car, Tyler appeared from around the corner of the house. A lanky cat trotted a few steps behind her but froze when it saw Jonas and then darted off.

Jonas strode forward to greet her. "Tyler, it's good to see you again. Sorry to put you out on such short notice."

She came up to him and gently slapped her hand on the hood of the vehicle. "Isn't this method of arrival a little old-fashioned for you, Jonas? Or are you just trying to fit in with the atmosphere?" Her smile carried a hint of self-mockery.

"I guess I'd need a horse and buggy for that, wouldn't I?" Jonas said a little too loudly, his attempt at lightness sounding false. More quietly, he added, "Anyway, I figured you wouldn't like a helo giving fits to the wildlife."

Tyler made only a vague sound of acknowledgment. She stood there for a few moments, abstracted, sorting Jonas' mood. It was as present to her as the sight and sound of him. He was deeply unsettled, and by something far more pervasive than simple nervousness. Although what exactly was troubling him she could not yet tell. A flicker of embarrassment passed over him. She looked at him sympathetically. "Certain perceptions," she hung a trace of irony on the word, "get in the way of small talk."

"Yeah, I guess."

She turned and led the way toward the house. "Mind sitting outside?" she asked. Out of politeness, she had made it a question.

"No, that'd be fine. I'd like it."

At the back of the house was a small flagstone patio shaded by old trees and furnished with a table and chairs. Tyler and Jonas sat at the table which was made of weathered wood. The chairs were the same and unpadded but comfortable nonetheless. On the table was a current generation apps pad, a pitcher of water, two tall and two short glasses, an insulated container of ice, and a bottle of brandy. Expensive brandy, Jonas noted. And chosen for his preference.

Tyler filled the taller glasses with ice and water. Into each of the others she poured a generous measure of brandy.

"Did you think I was going to need this?" Jonas said as he took the brandy from her.

"Well, the ambience is wrong. It ought to be gin and tonic or maybe a mint julep." Jonas made a face. Tyler took the other glass of brandy and sipped a little. "Actually I do have the mint. Only I can't swear the cats haven't been at it." She smiled.

"I'll survive on this, thanks." Jonas lifted his glass and took an appreciative swallow.

Tyler watched him assessingly. She had known Jonas a long time, since he had been a staff psychologist for the Department of Psyonic Management. He had moved rapidly into administrative positions and a little over two years ago he had been selected to head the department. He had been appointed Commissioner for Psyonic Management. His was one of the most ticklish of bureaucratic positions but he handled it well, managing to keep both psy perceivers and the general public reasonably content with the department's operations. He owed his success largely to two outstanding qualities. He had a careful, even skeptical, intellect coupled with an emotional balance which made diplomacy natural to him. Jonas was smart, steady, and sensible. Only right now, all that steadiness and sense were barely holding firm against an anxiety so deep it amounted almost to panic. It occurred to Tyler whatever he wanted from her, he wanted it very badly, and she wasn't going to like it.

"You know," he said at last, "I drove up here mostly because I thought it would help settle me down. I guess it didn't work." He drank a little more of his brandy. "I'm probably overreacting anyway." He looked at her, as if for confirmation. But Tyler simply waited.

She knew he was feeling a particular sense of awkwardness that was typical of conventional perceivers around psy perceivers. It was the discomfort of suspecting that everything you were about to say had been "heard" before you opened your mouth. Of course, Jonas knew better, but it still bothered him. Even with all his experience he could not help feeling that Tyler already knew everything he had come to say.

Tyler tried to ease him past his hesitation. "So far, Jonas, all I know is that you're worried, very worried. And I know what you're worried about has to do with psy perception. But then, I didn't need to sort that. I've known it since I got your call."

He knew she was trying to make things easier for him. "Yeah, I know, I know," he said. "It's just that I've been so taken up with this, it seems..." He broke off to smile lamely. "It seems you really ought to be able to read my mind."

She shrugged slightly. "Well, you've got the motto on your office wall," she said.

"Sure. Sure. You read books, not minds. I do try to remember." He took a long swallow of his brandy. "All right. Here goes." From the inside pocket of his jacket, Jonas pulled out a reader. Looking at Tyler's apps pad, he said, "Won't need that. Nothing on this," he waggled the reader, "can be transferred or downloaded." He tapped the reader and slid it across to Tyler. On view was a list of a names. Eight were grouped together, the ninth was set off from the others. Arranged in columns for each name was a date, a location, and a time. Jonas waited while Tyler looked over the display. Then he said,

"The dates are the dates those people died. The locations are where their bodies were found. The times are when."

Tyler noticed the earliest date was about five months ago, the middle of January. The last one, the one set off by itself, was for a man named Joleson Randle. His death had been reported at 4:47 a.m. on June 25th. This morning, in fact. In that respect, Randle's death conformed to the others on the list. They had all been discovered in the early morning hours, between three and six, with times of death estimated at six to seven hours earlier.

Tyler glanced at Jonas quizzically. There was no doubt this information was the source of his turmoil. But exactly why it was, she had not yet teased out of the tangled knots of his consciousness.

A few moments passed before Jonas finally said, "I got a call about this a couple of months ago, after the fifth death on the list here, from Isa Wilkins." Tyler nodded in recognition. Isa Wilkins was Operations Chief of Law Enforcement for Philly Sector. "He wanted me to be aware of something coming from Statistics and Probability. A possible problem that might be developing. These deaths were getting flagged. Everyone on this list was found dead, most of them in the street, a couple in back corridors of public buildings. Medical examiners reported in all cases that the deaths resulted from natural causes. The same natural causes." Jonas gestured toward the reader. "Everyone on this list dropped dead of some kind of stroke or cerebral hemorrhage. Only Stats and Prob didn't like those similarities two months ago, and they like them even less now.

"Given all the factors, medical history, genetics, statistical occurrences in the population at large, time and place of death, all the stuff they deal with, Stats and Prob have marked these deaths as highly questionable. They say it's unlikely this series could have occurred naturally and coincidentally.

"They're still running the statistical assessment on the last one, Randle. He was found by a garbage detail, by the way." Jonas allowed himself a tight smile, acknowledging the irony. "They'll probably have it by the time I get back. Anyway if his death conforms, which I suspect it will, they'll have nine in the cluster and a probability rating that's just about in the range for initiating a police investigation." He looked at Tyler to see if he had provoked a reaction in her.

Tyler frowned and said, "They really suspect these deaths could be homicides? Despite the findings of the medical reports."

Jonas shrugged. "Stats and Prob are always circumspect about how they word their reports. They never actually say it that way. They limit themselves to the negative. What they've told Wilkins is that it's unlikely these deaths could have...and I quote, 'spontaneously resulted from the apparent natural causes.'"

Jonas' initial anxiety had calmed somewhat as he gave his account, but the emotion Tyler had sorted from him originally seemed to be resurfacing. All he had said so far had been preliminary. It was interesting certainly, but it didn't explain why Wilkins had brought this matter to Jonas and why Jonas had brought it to her. And now that Jonas was almost to the heart of the matter, he hesitated again.

Tyler watched him as he fiddled with his glass, rolling it between his hands. "Jonas," she prompted.

He sat staring down at the glass. Then he looked up and said, "Wilkins called me on this for a couple of reasons. One is most of the people on this list had some affiliation with anti-psy groups. Mostly memberships in one of the major loudmouth organizations. The Thought Protectors, Guardians of Privacy, that kind of thing." The distaste in Jonas was evident as he spoke. "No real significant involvement. At least nothing on record. Just card carriers, as far as anyone can tell. You know."

Tyler waited without saying anything. Jonas was almost to his point. Too quickly, he finished the rest of his brandy, then set his glass down and pushed it away. "The main reason Wilkins contacted me is because they've run into problems with method. Namely, they couldn't come up with any. No known way these strokes or hemorrhages could have been induced. On the one hand, the Prob analysis indicates the deaths weren't simply natural and coincidental, instead indicates these people were probably murdered. On the other, they can't figure out how anyone could have done it. All the deaths appear to have simply resulted from a spontaneous brain hemorrhage."

As Jonas had gone on speaking, Tyler had gradually sorted enough from him to get some idea where he was going, of the core of his turmoil, but she held silent to let him continue.

"Anyway, they ran some hypotheticals as they always do in such cases." Jonas had been looking in Tyler's direction but without any focus beyond his words. Suddenly he really looked at her. She could see her own intentness mirrored in him. "By this point, I don't guess I have to tell you, do I," he said and then, in a rush as if he wished to disown the words even as he spoke them, "a hypothetical for psyonic impartment as a possible method correlated on all points."

Jonas' agitation bubbled up and he could no longer sit still. He got up restlessly and walked to the edge of the shade cast by the big old trees which surrounded Tyler's house. Tyler followed his gaze across the fields where the late afternoon summer sunlight had mixed green and gold with its peculiar intensity. Two horses grazed peacefully in the nearer field. But she knew Jonas really didn't see the calm beauty laid out before him. He had attention only for his own thoughts. Abruptly he turned around and said, "Of course, it's purely hypothetical."

For Jonas, the solace went no deeper than the spoken words. It fascinated Tyler that in his mind the hypothesis already had the force of fact, despite the strong overlay of denial in him. And it was to that certainty she responded. "Maybe so, but it doesn't *seem* hypothetical to you, Jonas."

"Damn it, Tyler..."

"There's no sense in ignoring what I know to be true."

Jonas came back to the table. He picked up one of the glasses of ice water and took a long drink. Putting the glass down, he pulled one of the chairs off to the side and sat, his legs stretched out in front of him. "OK, Tyler, tell me what I'm feeling."

"Private non-psy analysts get, how much for doing that? Six, seven hundred dollars an hour."

Although he was sitting sideways to her, Tyler could see Jonas' thin smile. "Cute," he said. "You think you've calmed the patient down enough?" He turned to look at her.

"It's a peculiar state of mind, Jonas. The more you want to resist believing in a possibility, the more your mind decides the reason you're fighting it is that it might be true." Even as she spoke, Tyler knew she had been concentrating on Jonas' reaction partly as a way of avoiding her own. Murder by psy impartment. It sounded like a blurb for a quikvid thriller, and seemed about as likely. Not that there hadn't been speculation ever since impartment had been identified.

Impartment was the rarest form of psy function. It was quite literally the ability to place or impart unspoken words into someone else's mind. But even psy perceivers who had demonstrated that ability almost never used it. Mastering and maintaining the extremely focused concentration it required was just too difficult, especially when there didn't seem to be much point to it.

Tyler thought about her first experience with impartment. It had happened when she was a young child and she couldn't actually remember the event which triggered it. She recalled it at all only because of its later significance. What she remembered was being very afraid of something, calling out for help and being heard, even though she hadn't called aloud. As she grew older, she came to understand what the adults around her had known. In her childhood terror she had used impartment.

Years later when it was time to receive an official control factor rating, she had been asked to try to demonstrate that ability again. At first, it had seemed impossible, but then she'd managed it. Wryly she remembered what, in her frustration, she had imparted to the examiner.

--It's too damn much trouble.--

And it had been. However, over time, impartment had become less difficult. But using it never came to seem less stressful and, the effort involved aside, Tyler was never comfortable with it.

Probably as she well knew, not so much because of the energy it took, but because conventional perceivers viewed impartment with such suspicion. For it was not only the most uncommon psy capability, it was also the most intrusive. And her own reaction to impartment was largely a reflection of the feelings of the non-psy around her. Looking back on her experiences with it, she knew she had been trained to the notion that impartment was something better left alone.

Chapter Three

"Tyler." Jonas' voice cut across her reflections. He had sat upright and was watching her closely. "I thought I'd lost you completely."

Tyler pulled her attention back to him. "Well, you did drop something on me, you know."

Jonas said, "It really doesn't make any sense, does it? Thinking someone to death." He tried to smile but it didn't quite come off.

"No," she said abruptly. To temper her brusqueness, she added. "At least, not in terms of my experience. Still there have been arguments made that it's theoretically possible."

Jonas sprawled back in his chair again. "Well, I don't believe it's possible. At least that's what I believe in my head. No matter what you say I'm feeling." He sounded almost petulant.

"Yet you're here, Jonas."

"Yeah, that's because it's not what I believe that really matters. How'd you like to see this spreading through the blogs like a virus? 'Government report cites probability of psyonic murder spree.'" He jerked upright again. "Can you imagine the reaction to that? The great public out there isn't going to worry about fine distinctions between hypotheticals and the actual unlikelihood of the possibility being suggested. This business, handled wrong, could be the worst bombshell in relations between psy and conventional perceivers since the existence of psy perception was verified."

As he spoke, an image rose unbidden in Jonas' mind. It took shape and he could not dispel it. A street. In the background a red glow as if fires were burning somewhere. In the foreground a person crouched in the shelter of a wall, the face distorted with fear. Unseen but clearly heard, the rumbling and tramp of a mob, intent on murder. And then suddenly the mob had closed upon its prey. There was a brief surge of movement, the mob drew back. At the base of the wall, no longer sheltering, lay a body, torn and bloody.

Abruptly Jonas flung himself forward, so that his elbows rested on his thighs. With the suddenness of his movement, the picture in his mind finally broke but he knew Tyler had sorted it. His hands, which had been tightly clenched, hung limp. He blew out an exasperated breath. "I said it before. I know I'm overreacting."

Jonas didn't notice but Tyler flinched as if suddenly startled. She had been lost in the image that had dominated him, an image of rioting mobs intent on killing psy perceivers. It had been melodramatic, even outlandish. But it was also obvious, for Jonas, it was an image that had plagued him repeatedly, an image he could not ignore. He both believed it and didn't believe it. His ambivalence heightened, not reduced, the emotional intensity it produced. Tyler pulled herself back from the image and the emotion it had provoked. Very dryly, she said, "Overreacting? I certainly hope so."

Jonas seemed not to have heard her. He was still intent on his own thoughts. "And yet..." he began, but stopped. He straightened up and deliberately spread his fingers across his knees as if trying to find composure in the gesture. He looked down for a moment, then abruptly he turned his chair around to face Tyler again. He took another gulp of water and said, "So, anyway, that's why I'm here. To ask you to help."

Tyler nodded but it was a confirmation of expectations not an agreement. She could feel her own reluctance and resistance and she regretted that Jonas could not. "Just what is it you want me to do, Jonas?"

Trying to keep his voice level, he began, "If this series of deaths continues, the probability is going to move right up into the certainty zone. If that happens, Wilkins is going to have to open an official homicide investigation. Only given the problem of method, he isn't going to be able to treat this case as a simple matter of sector jurisdiction. He'll have to take it to Policy and over there Rackland isn't even going to come close to messing around with any possible violations of the Internal Security Act. He'll call in CBI." The more explanation and build up Jonas provided, the more Tyler knew she really wasn't going to be happy about what he wanted when he finally got to it. "If it goes to Central Bureau, it's going to be all but impossible to keep this thing under wraps. Not with Hardin Toller's contacts there."

"What do you want me to do?" Tyler asked again.

Jonas heard the edge in her voice and sighed. "I've got a meeting set up with Chief Wilkins for tomorrow afternoon. I'd like you to be present at that." Jonas was still stalling, avoiding the point. But even as he did so, Tyler finally sorted something specific from him. A name surfaced. And then another.

This time her impatience got the better of her. She didn't wait for Jonas to speak the names. "What's Laurence got to do with this? Or Dorian Rath, for that matter," she demanded.

Disconcerted, Jonas blurted out, "I wish you wouldn't do that."

"Hard not to. Sometime." Tyler spoke with no trace of apology. "Especially when you keep putting off what you want to say."

"OK. Wilkins and I...well, I've persuaded the Chief to have you...sound the two of them out, I suppose you'd say, before we try to decide what to do next. If you're willing."

"You seem to have missed a step, Jonas."

Jonas nodded unhappily. "Yeah, I guess." Still uneasy about what he had to tell her, he went on, "As soon as Stats and Prob calculated the hypothetical, naturally they began to run checks on all resident CF4s, as well as nonresidents who were in metro at the relevant times. The preliminary report identifies Laurence Meredith and Dorian Rath as...what's the term they use? Available to be suspects. In this case that means they were in metro at the time of all the deaths and their movements can't be verified completely enough to rule them out."

"Are they the only two?"

"So far. Fortunately most of the sector resident CF4s don't live or work in central metro. We've got most of them eliminated."

"Like me, Jonas." The edge in Tyler's voice had grown sharper.

"You know I had you checked first thing."

"Pity you're not permitted twenty-four hour tracking surveillance on us, isn't it?"

"Come on, Tyler," Jonas protested. She made an impatient brushing motion with her hand, but whether to wave away Jonas' remonstrance or her own sarcasm was not clear. He went on insistently, "The first thing we've got to do is eliminate the registered CF4s. In case this thing continues to escalate. I think you can give us some guidance on how to proceed with Laurence and Dorian, whether to consider them," he hesitated over the words, "genuine suspects or not." Tyler grimaced. Responding to her displeasure, Jonas urged, "The Chief's willing to sit on this as long as he can. By rights he could have taken it to Rackland already, spread the responsibility. But he hasn't. He doesn't mind carrying the load when there's a lot at stake, but with this one he needs help, our help." Jonas felt he had pleaded his case, but he wasn't sure he had pleaded it well. Tyler caught the uncertainty in him, but she waited, unresponsive, her face blank. Jonas fidgeted uncomfortably. Finally he asked, "Will you do it? Will you work with me...with us...on this?"

Tyler continued without expression. After a long pause, she asked, "Is it a Demand, Jonas?"

"Does it have to be?"

A Demand, the government's special claim on the cooperation of a "group of citizens of unusual capabilities who shall in extraordinary circumstances give such aid and service as is necessary to further justice, promote the general welfare, and contribute to national security." Tyler had always found the echoes of the original source in the wording highly ironic. The full text of the law was carefully detailed and set forth the parameters under which the government could act to enforce its terms. But there was no question, given the circumstances he had outlined, Jonas would be able to make a case for calling a Demand. It would take a little more time and it would increase the risk of publicity. But it would be the official, correct way to proceed.

All that, of course, was exactly what Jonas wanted to avoid. He wanted her help but he wanted it unofficially, without being required to call a Demand. And in this case, that made good sense. Tyler conceded the point and resented it at the same time. Panicky and anxiety ridden Jonas might be, nonetheless he understood those feelings were his strongest allies in getting what he had come for. Especially that image of riot and destruction which glimmered in his mind like a fell light and which he could not shake off no matter how much he chided himself for overdramatizing. And which now Tyler could not shake off either.

So what was there to say in answer to his question, does it have to be a Demand?

"No, Jonas. It doesn't."

"Tyler, I..."

"No speeches. What you're asking me to do is spy on Laurence and Dorian. I don't want to do it, I resent doing it. But I will. Let's just leave it at that."

Jonas could not quite suppress a sigh. He had accomplished what he came for. He felt relief, but he felt guilt as well.

Tyler sorted both emotions. "That's what makes you so lethal, Jonas," she said.

He knew she was reacting to what he felt, so he looked a little sheepish. "What?'

"That sincere and touching quality of regretting the leverage you use to gain your results."

He shrugged. "The only leverage I use is what I honestly feel."

"Exactly. And that's what gives you the advantage." He started to say something, but Tyler didn't wait for him. "So what do you have in mind? I call Laurence and Dorian and say let's have a little chat about the possibility of murder by psy impartment."

Jonas ignored her sarcasm. "First thing, we meet with Chief Wilkins tomorrow. Go over things with him. Give him a chance to ask you any questions he might have, add anything to what I've already told you. Then, I don't suppose you've noticed, but Friday's the night of the reception which kicks off the annual APCU conference."

Tyler frowned slightly. "I got the invitation. I didn't pay any attention to the date." APCU was the acronym for the Association to Promote Cooperative Understanding, a well-meaning group which worked to encourage more social interaction between psy perceivers and conventionals. It had long been fashionable with upper middle class liberals. Tyler's name was kept on their membership list by virtue of an annual contribution, but it had been a long time since she had attended any of their functions.

"Everybody will be there," Jonas went on. "More to the point, Laurence and Dorian will be there."

"And you want me to be there, too," Tyler said sourly.

"It's the perfect opportunity," Jonas said with an attempt at enthusiasm.

Tyler looked at him doubtfully. "Don't you think my turning up is going to be a bit conspicuous? I haven't been to any events like that in a couple of years."

But Jonas only said, "Well, we've got to start someplace. And we really don't have time to plan anything more subtle."

Tyler glanced over the list on the reader again. "You really think more of these...unsatisfactory deaths...are going to show up?"

"I don't know. All I do know is I can't afford to wait and find out." Jonas retrieved the reader. He stood up. "So, I guess we're settled," he finished, with more assurance than he felt.

Tyler rose as well and they walked around the front of the house to the car. The lanky cat Jonas had seen when he arrived was now sprawled on the hood. It looked up lazily at their approach. Noticing Jonas, it rose lithely to its feet, sprang off the car, and sat at some distance staring at them.

"Skittish," Jonas said.

"Cautious," Tyler countered.

Jonas looked at her. "By the way, don't worry about your location order. I'll have Cal take care of it. We'll just put 'research' as the reason for you spending a few days in metro." Searching his memory, Jonas grew thoughtful. "You don't come in much anymore, do you? And it *has* been awhile since you attended anything like the APCU reception."

"I guess." Tyler's tone was uncharacteristically vague.

Jonas thought a little harder. "In fact it was my investiture as commissioner. That's over two years ago." Jonas opened the door and lowered himself into the driver's seat. "You are becoming pretty reclusive, you know."

"Occupational hazard. Besides you should be thankful. Otherwise I might have been in metro when one of your problem corpses turned up. Then where would you be?"

"Tyler, I do appreciate this," Jonas said. It was an indirect apology.

"I'll see you tomorrow. In metro."

Chapter Four

Jonas left in time to catch the light for the drive back. After he had gone, Tyler went in, called the Fuentes to let them know she'd be away for a few days, and packed.

She went to her study and stood for a while, contemplating whether to download to her apps pad the files for the book she was working on. She was about halfway through a draft, at a point in which she seemed to live more in the world she was writing than in the world of external realities. It was an awkward place for an interruption. Finally she decided to bring along the last two chapters she had drafted. Not that she really expected to get any serious work done. She doubted there'd be room for the kind of concentration it needed. She just hoped Jonas' estimate that she'd be gone only a few days would turn out to be accurate. When she had finished in the house, she went back outside to watch dusk deepen into night and to think.

To think about Jonas' bombshell, the possibility of murder by impartment. She had the curious split feeling that comes when the information you've absorbed is at odds with your sense of its reality. She noted with interest that in part she simply discounted the whole thing. Believed Jonas was right when he said he was overreacting, even though for him those protestations were insincere. Saw as incredible and unsubstantial the leap from a series of deaths with a questionable probability to the use of impartment as a murder weapon. Some part of her insisted on treating everything Jonas had said as a theory, and not a particularly reasonable one at that. In time, and with time enough, Stats and Probability would come up with the actual solution to the problem of the unlikely sequence of deaths.

Tyler knew that without psy perception this skeptical and sensible reaction would have dominated over her other one, the one which took Jonas' worries very seriously indeed, which believed them the way he did, despite his resistance and protestations to the contrary.

But then as she had told Jonas, he had the advantage over her in that. Like most people who were non-psy he couldn't really understand that. If there was one fairly consistent opinion about psy perception by people who didn't have it, it was to view it as a source of power, of control, over others. It had never seemed that way to Tyler, no more than seeing something gave you power over it. Rather the other way around in fact.

And so it was with Jonas' feelings. Tyler knew, directly knew, how Jonas was reacting to the situation he had laid out for her. And it was that knowledge which made it impossible for her to reason away Jonas' fears. Throughout their conversation, Jonas had been flooded with anxiety. His efforts at calm had seemed increasingly like a tired swimmer desperately trying to tread water. In his generalized distress, the graphic image of rioting mobs surfaced no matter how hard he tried to push it away. He really believed, quite against his will, that this matter could spark a fierce outbreak of civil unrest and mob violence. All directed at psy perceivers.

Of course, it was impossible to know how likely it was for such a chilling vision to come true. Maybe just the suspicion of a series of murders by means of impartment wouldn't be enough to set off anti-psy riots. But it would probably be enough to add considerable weight to the negative side of the ambivalence most people had toward psy perception, an ambivalence which sprang from an immediate personal response. Whenever Tyler found herself in the presence of a non-psy, she always sorted in the other a sense of disquiet that surfaced, no matter how briefly. Even Jonas experienced that little ripple, amounting almost to fear, when he first found himself in her company. And she knew that other psy found the same reaction in conventional perceivers.

Still, for the most part, the general population took the existence of psy perception for granted. The midrange of public opinion held the position that yes, there were psy perceivers, but their numbers were too small to be of major concern. "Statistically insignificant" was the phrase Tyler remembered. Moreover most people felt there were enough safeguards to protect "normal" citizens from any unusual advantage individual psy perceivers might otherwise have. Psy perceivers were registered, rated, and required by law to submit to regular profile examinations which confirmed that they fell within the accepted norms of psychological stability. They were also barred from certain professions. But most comforting of all to conventionals, psy perceivers were easily identified. A registered psy's control factor was a matter of public record and was also included on the national ID commcard everyone carried.

But there was also a minority opinion. Some people considered the very existence of psy capability an unacceptable intrusion on the basic core of human experience, the privacy of thoughts and feelings. And Tyler could literally understand how they felt. Enough people felt that way for there to be more than one group which lobbied strenuously for greater restraints on the civil liberties of psy perceivers, groups like the ones the victims, if that's what they were, had belonged to.

Undoubtedly the Stats and Prob report itself, no matter what else came of this business, could have political repercussions. If, into the current mixed bag of public opinion, you dropped a probability assessment that suggested maybe someone was using impartment to kill people... Tyler was fascinated to find her thought breaking off as if it had run into a wall. She didn't even want to let herself consider it.

And that was contemplating an impact on more or less mainstream political opinion. There were still others, people whose fear and distrust of psy perceivers was deep and all consuming. The lunatic fringe, as Jonas invariably called them. Maybe they were that.

They had no faith that the law could protect them from psy perception which they viewed as an ever-present threat. They were convinced that substantial numbers of psy perceivers avoided detection and registration and lurked among them, sorting what they thought and felt and using that special knowledge to gain incalculable advantage. Their fears might be groundless, but they were insistently real, as Tyler knew from her own experience whenever she had encountered someone who felt that way.

What such people didn't understand was that when confronted with such hatred the typical reaction for a psy perceiver was avoidance, retreat from the pervasive emotional unrest which dominated such people.

And that's what was so appalling about Jonas' case. If this crazy theory of murder by impartment were true, then maybe the crazy fears of the lunatic fringe weren't so crazy. And that was a thought which Tyler could not fit comfortably into her understanding at all.

She let herself explore that reaction. There was more to her resistance than trying to avoid the fears of doom and destruction weighing on Jonas. To communicate some of what she felt, she had been tempted to use impartment herself in her conversation with him. She had wanted to plant in his mind a resounding --NO-- to his request for her help so he would fully grasp how deep her aversion to the whole business was. But she had known she was going to agree and it had seemed pointless to add to Jonas' troubles. He had enough to deal with.

And that was exactly the problem. Tyler could not conceive how a psy who was high range enough to have impartment capability could ignore the inevitable empathy psy perception brought. Short of an act of direct and even desperate self-defense, it did not seem possible that a psy perceiver could kill in that way. For the psy perceiver would share with an immediacy that could not be evaded what the victim was experiencing.

And Tyler knew her musings had come full circle. The advantage, Jonas, lies with you, with your kind, she thought. I know what you feel, but you cannot reciprocate. You think you understand my reluctance to do what you asked, but you don't. For myself, I might have been able to deny the abstract claims of civic responsibility, but I can't turn away from the insistent reality of *your* experience. Because I do know how you feel.

Long after dark, Tyler continued to sit in the quiet, familiar surroundings of the isolation she had cultivated. Looking out across what in the late afternoon had been a green-gold field, now she saw only the blackness of a country night, punctuated but not lit by great luminous fireflies.

FYEO
To: D. Hollins Riscoll
From: Carla Jamal, Chief of Staff
October 5, 2022

Re: Proposed legislation HB 163.458

It looks like a no go with regard to any compromise on making psy status public. Even the moderates and moderate to liberals are unwilling to take to their constituents any package that does not include a disclosure provision. The essence of it is this: no one wants a mind reader for a neighbor without having the means to find out about it.

The general consensus is, in addition to a legal requirement for registration, we need psy control factor rating included as part of the individual identity record, with that information provided on the national ID card and accessible through on-line public records. There's also a pretty strong minority faction pushing for some more noticeable 'badge.' Charlie Hapwood suggests a collar or lapel pin would be 'tasteful and reassuring.' His words. But I think, as long as we agree to public disclosure of psy status, Hapwood and his group will probably give in on anything further, at least as regards legal requirements. But you'd probably have to fight a bit.

As for singling out the psy population for specific attention with the attendant civil liberties and discrimination issues which loom so large in your thinking, these do not carry enough weight with the other members whose support you're seeking. The counter arguments about the uniqueness of the situation and the need to protect the right to privacy of the normal population overshadow all other considerations for them.

And let's face it, DH, the members are well aware that there's little risk involved in taking a firm line on this. Given all statistical indications, the actual number of psy perceivers will continue to be too small to generate any significant political force. And therefore they're unlikely to pose a political threat.

Turning to the subject of proscribed occupations, once again support for the concept is virtually unanimous. Substantial agreement exists for keeping psy perceivers out of certain professions. For obvious reasons law enforcement, the judiciary, trial attorneys head the list. There is also strong support to ban psy from instructional positions in public education, at least at the primary and secondary levels. The argument seems to be along the lines of, "My constituents don't want their tax dollars used to force them to expose their children and their households to daily invasions of privacy." I think they believe psyonic teachers would find out all their dirty little secrets. Anyway we have been able to limit this push to the public sector, leaving private education untouched by this form of hysteria. There is room to negotiate with regard to positions in public universities and community colleges.

There's been very little discussion about elective office because no one seems to have any worries that a psy perceiver would ever get elected to anything. But again that ties in to the general insistence that all telepathic members of the population be clearly identified as such. (Of course, the projected psychological profile and control factor rating systems are seen as key components in the entire package.)

Fortunately it looks like we're going to be able to steer clear of terms like 'mind reading' or 'psyching.' Everyone seems pretty comfortable writing the bill with the more neutral terminology which has come into use for the most common psy functions: 'sorting' for the ability of psy perceivers to make sense out of the perceptions available to them, 'closure' for the ability to shut out psy perception, 'screening' for the process by which one psy regulates or blocks the sorting capability of another.

One last thing. There's definitely been a feeler from Durkin's office. It seems like he's got some deal in mind, something hooked up with a pet idea he has. His staff, I talked to Jay Collins, are keeping it pretty vague, but it seems the grand old man has some notion about a form of drafting psy perceivers to some kind of public service, either a specific term or on demand as needed. I get the impression they're waiting for you to respond to the tentative overture before they spell anything out. I don't need to tell you how important Durkin's switch would be, so I won't. It would mean six or seven votes at least. (All right, I said I wouldn't tell you, but I did.)

Well, that's about it. I know you won't be pleased with a lot of it, but I think for any package to have a realistic chance, we'll have to include the items I've discussed here, including Durkin's brainstorm, whatever it turns out to be.

Chapter Five

The day after Jonas' visit, Tyler was met at Philly TransPort by Jonas' administrative assistant. He had alert blue eyes set in a pleasant face. A swatch of sandy colored hair fell across his forehead. He was young, ambitious, and also a very skillful CF3. He'd been with Jonas just over a year and a large part of his duties consisted in riding point for Jonas in his dealings with other psy perceivers. He extended his hand and Tyler took it. "T. West? Commissioner Acre asked me to look out for you. I'm Calvin Houlston."

"Yes, I know," she said. "Please, Tyler's fine."

"Thanks. And it's Cal, of course."

He led the way to Clearance. Tyler copied her entry permit from her apps pad to the TransPort commsys. They watched the permit come up on the display panel. Under purpose for entry it read: Research and Consultation, Department of Psyonic Management.

Tyler let a raised eyebrow image form. "That," she nodded at the display, "should cover every eventuality."

"We thought it would." Cal managed a trace of a smile but his smile didn't match his mood. "Jonas has gone on to Enforcement. He'll meet you there."

Something behind the matter of fact statement caught Tyler's attention. "They confirmed Randle, didn't they?"

Cal cleared his throat. "Yeah. Jonas and Chief Wilkins will give you all the details."

They looked at each other, each knowing the other was sorting a similar blend of worry and denial. There didn't seem to be anything worth saying so Cal led the way to the pedestrian strip which would carry them to the main concourse and the exit.

Cal turned to say something when he suddenly realized Tyler was no longer beside him. He looked around to find her. She had stepped off the strip and was standing very still. He hurried back, but as he approached he could sort nothing from her. Her screening was too tight. "Are you all right, T. West?"

A few seconds passed before she answered. "Yes." But she still stood there, as if waiting for something. What she felt but screened from Cal was the rush of a familiar and unpleasant sensation which, for some years now, she always experienced when she first returned to metro. It was a vague sense of unease, almost a kind of mental queasiness. Motion sickness of the mind. She had expected it, but she had forgotten how strong that feeling of disquiet was. Or maybe it was stronger than it used to be.

But all she said to Cal by way of explanation was, "I just don't like crowds very much." Tyler returned to the pedestrian strip. Cal followed her. As they continued toward the exit, Tyler sorted a reaction from her companion. He thought it really wasn't very crowded in the Port today, but he was too polite to say it. So Tyler added, "Jonas says I should get in more often. Not spend so much time in country solitude. Maybe he's right."

Cal was embarrassed that she had picked up his fleeting thought. "I guess I better upgrade my screening around you," he said apologetically.

When they exited the concourse, Cal led the way to an unmarked ceevee. He entered their destination into the guidance system, and the vehicle glided smoothly off. They rode awhile in silence, each wrapped in their own thoughts. Then Tyler said, "You've met him."

"Who, Chief Wilkins? Yeah."

"What's he like?"

"He's OK. A good cop, a role he's proud of. But he's a good administrator, too. Surprisingly so, especially for an Operations guy."

After a short pause, Cal added, "Above all, lots of savvy. Not just about police work. Politically as well."

"He seems to be pretty considerate of Jonas' worries in this matter."

"Wilkins is not just a functionary, you know. It matters to him, the public welfare, I guess you'd say. And I think he has a better than average understanding of what you call Jonas' worries. Besides he agrees with Jonas. He believes it's in the public interest to keep this business as contained as possible. Believes it strongly enough to run a few risks." Cal thought for a moment. "Still with the addition of Randle, we're getting close to a point where he's not going to have much choice in the matter." They both thought about that for a while. Just before they pulled into Enforcement, Cal raised the question that had hung unasked between them. "You think it's possible? Killing someone psyonically."

"I've been trying to decide how I'm going to answer that when Wilkins asks it." Tyler allowed herself a meager smile. "So far I haven't got much further than I'm not sure." She looked at Cal assessingly. "And you? What do you think? Is it possible?"

"No," Cal said emphatically. "Of course, I don't have direct experience with impartment." He left 'like you' unspoken. It seemed to be a cue for Tyler to elaborate. When she didn't, Cal added, "But either way, that damn Stats and Prob report is a problem. It needs to be negated. Fast."

Cal left Tyler at Enforcement saying he would meet Jonas at Psy Management later. That he and Jonas both felt Chief Wilkins would be more comfortable with only one psy perceiver present at their meeting.

Tyler walked into the reception area of the building which was the administrative center for Philly Sector Enforcement, an over large space that dwarfed the benches where people waited on whatever business had brought them there. It had the tacky grandeur typical of public buildings. Ceiling, walls, and floor of synthetic marble, all of which were dull and grimy with age. A maintenance worker slowly made the rounds picking up trash.

Tyler presented herself at the high counter with its polymeth plastic barrier that ran along the wall opposite the entry way. It was staffed by consciously polite people, armed and in full uniform. She, of course, was not directed to any of the waiting benches. An officer was summoned and she was escorted through one of the sets of security doors on either side of the reception desk. As she followed the officer through the door, she caught a faint reaction from the benches behind her. Someone wondered, with a little bitterness and a lot of resignation, who she was and what importance she had to expedite her admission. Or at least those were the words in which Tyler dressed the feeling she had sorted.

The office she was shown to was obviously where the Chief actually worked. Its furnishings were efficient rather than ceremonial. A large flat panel, flanked by windows, hung on the back wall. Beneath it was a work station. On its top surface, a couple of smaller panels rose on pedestals. A moderate desk faced the door, comfortable chair behind, two others facing it. In a corner to the right of the door four more chairs were grouped around a low table. A small cluster of photographs, certificates, and awards hung on the wall in that corner. Otherwise the walls were bare of decoration.

Jonas was standing as Tyler walked in and Chief Wilkins came around the desk to greet her. Jonas made the introductions. He and Tyler sat down.

Out of uniform, Isa Wilkins would have looked like any other prosperous professional or bureaucrat. Physically he had none of the burly toughness which the title Chief of Police called to mind. Still he moved like a man fit and ready for action. He was probably ten years older than Jonas but his face was smooth and unlined. His skin was a rich medium brown, a shade or two darker than his eyes.

Tyler noted the physical details but only in passing. It was Wilkins' state of mind which commanded her attention. And there she sorted pretty much what she had expected. There was the familiar uncertainty of a conventional perceiver who wondered exactly what unknown signals he was sending. But for Wilkins it was more a curiosity than a worry. Far more important to him was a sense of needing to assess Tyler, of having allowed Jonas his way in calling her in, but doubt about the advisability of that action.

When Wilkins had reseated himself behind his desk, he folded his hands in front of him, looked at Tyler and said, "I don't mean to be unduly abrupt, but I'm sure I don't have to tell you. Jonas' suggestion to involve you in this doesn't have my wholehearted support."

"It doesn't have my wholehearted support either, Chief Wilkins," Tyler replied.

Wilkins glanced at Jonas who shrugged and smiled weakly. Then Wilkins turned his gaze back to Tyler. "It's not that I don't appreciate your cooperation. I suppose we could say that none of us feels we have much choice. That irregular procedures are better than none." He waited as if to allow a response, but Tyler didn't say anything. After a brief pause, there was a perceptible shift in his focus, a sense that minor preliminaries were over and could now give way to more substantial matters. "I know Jonas has given you at least a brief outline of what we know, but there are things we certainly need to discuss in greater detail."

Tyler jumped to the first point of discussion. "The body you found yesterday. Cal Houlston told me. It fits the pattern."

"Yes, I'm afraid it does." Chief Wilkins tapped the apps pad that lay before him on his desk. On the large flat panel behind him, Jonas' list of the previous day appeared. Wilkins swivelled his chair to face it and said, "This latest death, same as the others. Cerebral hemorrhage, no previous medical indications. In conjunction with the full range of variables which the Stats and Probability people play around with, what we've got, as of Randle, is a negative probability of 6.92 that these deaths happened naturally and coincidentally." Jonas shifted uncomfortably but Wilkins continued smoothly. "Which is another way of saying that Stats and Probs suggest almost a seventy percent chance these nine deaths were...arranged."

Jonas shook his head. "Have they come up with any kind of link at all, Isa?"

"Not really, nothing solid anyway. Six out of the nine had memberships in the better known anti-psy organizations. That's a considerably higher than average percentage. All of them were at the lower end of the economic scale. A couple had continuous but marginal employment. Three of them had been on public assistance for some time. Three of them, not the same three, had police records. Minor stuff. Drunk and disorderly, barroom scuffles. That kind of thing."

Wilkins slid his finger across his apps pad. Screenfuls of information scrolled on the display panel. "It just goes on like that," he said. "No really significant pattern emerges, except for the anti-psy affiliations. Otherwise, the only other obvious link is that the list is skewed to the less prosperous end of the social scale." Wilkins let the display come to a halt and turned his chair back to face them. He looked at Jonas. "I've arranged clearance to have a copy of all this released to your department. If you think going over it in greater detail will help." He was skeptical that it would and not worried about showing it. "I don't have to tell you to be careful with it." He shifted his gaze to Tyler.

Jonas said, "Tyler will have this material in read only form." Wilkins nodded. Jonas added, "We don't expect to find what your analysts can't. Still, you never know."

Tyler had listened to Wilkin's summary and comments with no visible reaction. Now she said, "From what Jonas tells me, I understand motive is not really the prime concern at present."

Wilkins spread his hands in a gesture of acknowledgment. "Yeah, in a case like this, serial murders, if that's what they are." He shrugged. "You don't solve a case like this by motive. Motive, such as there is, is usually too irrational to be useful. As for opportunity, here it's open-ended. What this case hinges on," he paused to give weight to his words, "is method."

"And in this case, you don't have one," Tyler said.

Wilkins looked at her, his eyes large and bright. "None that we know of. Unless of course, you want to fool around with stuff like this." Without turning around, he pulled up a new display. On the wall panel appeared a series of IF-statements, each followed by its expansion code. Tyler didn't bother to cross reference those. Most of them were technical points she didn't have the expertise to evaluate. With the crucial expansion, the one which speculated on the possible use of impartment to commit murder, she was already familiar.

At the end of the list of IF-statements was the straightforward conclusion. Hypothesis of psyonic impartment as possible cause of death would meet the terms of all input variables submitted for the sequence under review.

Chapter Six

Tyler continued to look at the display, waiting for Wilkins to ask the question which was forming in his mind, the same one Cal Houlston had asked. At last, he did. "You think that's possible? You think someone could use impartment to kill somebody?"

Until the moment the question was asked, Tyler was sure her answer was still going to be, "I don't know." Nice, simple, noncommittal, and probably true. But suddenly that answer no longer seemed appropriate. Very deliberately and with an ability Tyler herself could not explain, she clearly directed into Chief Wilkin's mind the single word. --No.--

He jerked his head up. Simultaneously Tyler perceived a tremor of fear. However, Wilkins quickly recovered his composure.

Tyler looked at him almost defiantly. "That isn't the answer I'd planned," she said, "but I think I'll stand by it. For now, at least."

From Jonas there was perplexity for a moment, and then realization. He started to say something but Wilkins waved him off. "You did say you were bringing me someone who had some actual experience with this." Wilkins turned back to Tyler. "Jonas tells me you don't use that capability very often."

"No." Tyler searched around for an explanation, finding in herself even more reluctance than she had anticipated. "In the first place, it takes an unusual kind of concentration. I know I can achieve impartment, but it takes a lot of effort. Somehow it just doesn't seem worth it."

"It's more than that though, isn't it?" Wilkins asked. Tyler noticed that Jonas had again shifted position. She knew he felt like a concerned teacher watching a star pupil be examined.

"You noticed your own reaction," Tyler said. "Impartment makes people uncomfortable."

"Not just impartment, I think." Wilkins' tone was deceptively gentle. It masked an intentness which never seemed to leave him.

Tyler smiled. "Other forms of psy perception are a little easier for the recipient to ignore."

Wilkins nodded. "What you did. It was like somebody else suddenly being inside my head." He paused. "It gets your attention anyway. Which I suppose is what you had in mind."

"Actually it was the only way I could say 'no' and say it honestly." Tyler could feel the anticipation in both of them. "You both need to understand, ever since Jonas brought this to me, I've been trying to figure out what I really think about it. And I'm still not sure. If it were possible...somehow to..." Tyler found herself groping for words. "To feed not just words but...I don't know what you'd call it...an emotional overload into someone's mind, it does make me wonder what would happen. Whether it could make someone collapse...even die." She sorted a reaction of surprise from Jonas. And she answered it, even though he hadn't said anything. "You realize, I'm talking this out for the first time myself."

"You ever think of impartment in these terms? Before." It was the Chief who asked.

"No," Tyler said. "I've never thought of it as a weapon." She shook her head as if rejecting the idea. "What bothers me is that I can't imagine anyone seeing it through. You see, even if you could sustain it, you'd have to have such a level of involvement with your victims that it'd be almost like dying with them. At least, that's how it seems to me," she concluded. Even to herself she sounded defensive.

"I think I understand your point," Wilkins said cautiously. "But still, you don't feel it's an impossibility? This hypothesis."

"It's not that I can't accept the theoretical possibility, especially when you consider the strong negative reaction impartment always provokes," Tyler said, frowning. "It's just that I can't envision a psy perceiver going through what I think it would take to use such a capability. Not unless there was the most compelling reason. Certainly not for random and unmotivated killing."

Wilkins rubbed his fingers together. "Tell me, Tyler, if I had psy ability, would I sense some wishful thinking in all this."

"I've thought about that, too. A lot. I know I have strong incentives for wanting to reject all this. But I don't think my opinion is simply an act of denial on my part. Using impartment as a murder weapon, it just doesn't make sense to me." Sorting a mix of sympathy and scepticism from Wilkins, Tyler added with a sour smile, "Not when using more traditional methods would be so much easier. Unfortunately," she gestured toward the display, "all this data is a little hard to brush aside."

Wilkins ran his hand across the top of his head. "Yes, that does seem to be the problem we're stuck with." He stopped to consider the point they had reached. "I'm going to lay out some things. Just so we're all clear on where we stand.

"In the first place, the fact we're having this meeting, well, I hope that assures both of you I do understand how explosive this business could be. Right now, all of this, this report, and the indication of probable homicides, it's all still speculative. Still in a range that gives me some options, just barely. But," Wilkins turned specifically to Jonas, "at some point, if this series continues and the prob rating gets bad enough, gets to the point where the probability of homicide is all but certain, with no known method," he stopped for a moment, "then I'm going to have to share this with Rackland at Policy and that's going to bring CBI into it." Jonas leaned forward. Tyler could feel him searching for a response, but Wilkins didn't wait. "I know, Jonas. I know. Believe me, even for my own sake, I'd much rather handle this, whatever it is, through my own department. And I will as long as I can. I just want you to know, at some point, I'm probably going to run out of string."

"How long do you think we have, Isa?"

"One, two more. Unless we can come up with something to work on. You've got to understand, Jonas. It's not just that I'm in fear of the Internal Security Act. But if the Stats and Prob analysis is right, if this data really does reveal a series of homicides and worse, if someone like..." The Chief started to nod at Tyler but stopped himself. "If someone with T. West's level of psy ability is really using a form of psy perception to kill people...I can't let that happen. I can't leave my city at risk, threatened with something like that. And Policy Commissioner Rackland aside, if I feel I need the Central Bureau of Investigation, I'll call them in myself. No matter what the consequences for you."

Tyler could tell that feeding the Chief's intensity was a desire to be completely honest about what he could and would do. Because despite his words, he, like Jonas, was worried, deeply worried. And like Jonas, he desperately wanted this matter solved quietly and with no public outcry.

When Wilkins had finished his speech, he looked at both of them and said, "I just wanted you both to know."

No one said anything, but Tyler could feel the anxiety in both men, equally strong, but different, like two vivid but distinctive hues.

It was Tyler who broke the silence. "For my part, I'd like to know what you both expect from me at the reception tomorrow night."

"Yes, Jonas," Wilkins rejoined. "What do we expect?"

"It's what I told Tyler yesterday. We've got to start somewhere. As far as possible psy involvement goes anyway." Jonas turned to Tyler. "Obviously Isa and his people, they can handle normal investigative matters. But Laurence and Dorian, I'd really like something more concrete before the Chief calls either of them in under an official interrogatory."

Wilkins nodded glumly. "L. Meredith and D. Rath. We couldn't have two more high profile possibilities."

"Has your data search turned up anyone else?" Tyler asked.

"No. At present, they're the only two registered psy perceivers with a verified record of impartment capability whose presence in central metro at the time of all these deaths has been confirmed."

Tyler said, "So, you want me to see if I can sort anything. Anything from either of them that would justify calling them in with an interrogatory warrant." The other two might not be able to feel her distaste, but they could hear it in her words.

"I suppose there is another way to look at it," Wilkins said. "You could think of it as a way to rule either of them out."

"Frankly," Tyler said, "I doubt I'm going to produce much in the way of results one way or the other. After all, Dorian, Laurence, and I have about the same level of sorting and screening ability. I'm not going to get much, if anything, they don't want me to get. And I'll probably give away a little, too."

"I explained that to the Chief," Jonas said. "But if one of them is involved in this, that person already knows everything there is to know. And both of them do need to be checked." Jonas glanced at Wilkins, wanting confirmation. Wilkins nodded. Jonas swung back to Tyler. He continued insistently, "Look, the Chief and I know you can't deliver one of them on a platter. Or exonerate them. What I'm thinking of is...like in ordinary conversation. A gesture, a look, a tone of voice, it conveys more than the words say. That happens psyonically, too, doesn't it?"

"Yes," Tyler conceded.

"That's what I have in mind." Jonas paused looking for words which would match the determination he felt. "Your impression...something that would give us a clue of how to proceed with them."

Jonas and the Chief looked at her, waiting for her to restate her acceptance. "Yes, all right. I'll see what I can get for you." They both seemed satisfied, although in Jonas it was relief at exchanging a feeling of helplessness for some kind of action. In the Chief there was more a sense of skeptical pragmatism, a willingness to proceed without any great expectation of result. Tyler pondered their reactions. "There's another possibility we haven't mentioned." She knew very well that Jonas, at least, had thought of it and she guessed the Chief had, too.

Her guess was confirmed because it was Wilkins who responded. "An unregistered high level psy."

"I just don't think that's possible," Jonas said, a little too quickly.

Wilkins smiled with almost no change in the smooth brown contours of his face. "Stats and Prob don't agree with you, Jonas. It is possible. Not likely, but possible."

"I know what the stats say," Jonas said, denial still clear in his voice.

Tyler expelled a long breath. "It's a great choice, isn't it? What would you rather, Jonas? Your mad murderer be Laurence or Dorian. Or some unregistered psy." She regretted venting her frustration as soon as she did it, for that panicky under layer in Jonas swept across his consciousness. Wilkins looked at her inquisitively. Tyler answered his look. "I don't like spying on them for you. Laurence is a friend. Dorian, well...we rub each other the wrong way, but still...I don't like it."

Wilkins' expression became very serious. "Then why do it?" The question wasn't a challenge. He genuinely wanted to know.

Tyler thought about her answer and then said, "Because Jonas thinks it's necessary." She had picked her words carefully, wanting to see how the Chief would respond. He went immediately to the point.

"Do *you*...think it's necessary?"

"I think it's unavoidable."

Both Jonas and the Chief wanted to assign an officer to Tyler but she refused. And Jonas, sensing that she felt crowded, gave in without argument.

"I want you both to be cautious," Wilkins said. "Murderers have been known to turn on the people trying to track them down."

"If there is a murderer," Tyler said, "it isn't psy who are being killed."

"No, not yet."

As Jonas and Tyler left Enforcement headquarters, Jonas said, "I'll drop you at your hotel. Give us a chance to have a word on the way over." When they reached the ceevee, Jonas entered the destination program. Then he turned to Tyler. "Isa will give us all he can. I'm sure of that." Tyler nodded absently. "You surprised me, though. I didn't think you'd give him a sample of impartment unless..." Jonas' words trailed off.

"Unless you asked me, Jonas?" Tyler put a noticeable stress on the word 'asked.'

He shrugged. "Well, unless I suggested it, yeah. Tyler, I am sorry to involve you in all this."

"I meant it when I said it was unavoidable, Jonas. For both of us."

They had arrived at the hotel. As Tyler got out, Jonas leaned over and said, "Thanks, Tyler. For everything."

"Sure," she said. "But maybe you ought to wait to see how tomorrow turns out first."

Chapter Seven

By the end of the afternoon, Tyler found herself gratefully alone in the suite Jonas had reserved for her. The rooms held the sterile luxuriousness typical of expensive hotels. It was an atmosphere that usually provoked condescension from Tyler, but tonight she took solace from the feeling of isolation it gave her. She ordered a meal, ate, and then spent some time reviewing the files Jonas had transferred to the stand-alone reader he had this time let her keep. But if there was anything additional to be learned from them, whatever it was eluded her. Finally she gave up. She closed and blocked the files, then walked out onto the room's small balcony.

From this height, the city looked not only attractive but absolutely breathtaking. Directly below her spread the rectangle of Liberty Park. Framing it, buildings rose majestically above the tree tops. Beyond it, a broad avenue ran to the horizon. Along the avenue's wide pathway, the lights of Public Transport stops gleamed like jewels.

Tyler drew her gaze back along the length of the park. The park wasn't large, only two blocks wide by four blocks long, but it was a masterwork of reclaiming nature from the inexorable demands of concrete and steel. The tumbled heads of the trees tossing in the late afternoon wind looked like a green sea. She knew Jonas had selected this view, this proximity to the park, especially for her.

But as always, it seemed to Tyler these attractions were purchased by too great an expense of ugliness. Not many blocks from the park and the elegant streets below her were streets far more

48   *Psy Mind*

typical, streets like the ones the bodies had been found in. Narrow and gritty streets, where graffiti scrawled walls rose impersonally from the concrete in which they were planted. Where decrepit storefronts seemed left over from another time. Where discarded papers and containers blew along in the same wind that dusted the tree tops below. Tyler reflected that city dwellers never seemed to notice the general tackiness in which the occasional urban gem was set.

Her bleak response to the unnerving oppositions in the metro environment dovetailed exactly with her prevailing mood. The possibility of psyonic murder, the prospect of spying on Laurence and Dorian, those things could more than account for her gloom. But she knew her persistent feeling of depression had a deeper root. It grew from that undefinable level of psy awareness which had clicked in as soon as she had arrived in metro. It was the feeling which had caused her to startle Cal at the TransPort. The feeling was like the persistent rumble of bees working over meadow flowers. Or maybe like the restless heaviness before a summer storm. Whatever it was, it perplexed her. She could not account for it, nor dismiss it as imagination.

She knew it did not result from anything obvious, like an inability to sort the array of psy perceptions she picked up. She did that, as she always had, comfortably and naturally. This was something else, a faint buzz or hum at the back of her consciousness. Not intrusive enough to really get in the way and once she got used to it again, she wouldn't even notice it most of the time, but it would never completely leave her as long as she remained in metro. It was just another detail which made Jonas' unofficial request particularly irksome to her.

Breaking gently into Tyler's thoughts, a series of beeps came through the open door. She disliked boisterous ring tones. She walked back into the room and picked up her apps pad. She touched video and audio in but only audio out. Expecting either Jonas or Cal, she was surprised to see Laurence Meredith's image appear on the wall panel. At forty-two, he looked younger than his years. He had light brown skin, dark coffee-colored eyes, straight black brows, and crinkled black hair that hugged his head. But Tyler noticed his hair had become flecked with gray and the furrows that ran from his nose to the corners of his mouth seemed to have deepened since she saw him last. Still his handsome face held its familiar expression of wily observation

"Tyler, are you really in metro?" Laurence's tone of voice laughed at the question as he asked it.

Tyler turned on video out. "As you see. How did you know?"

Laurence grinned. "There are ways."

"Friends in high bureaucracies?"

"Let's just say Jonas isn't anymore shocked by my contacts in his office than I am by his in mine."

"You make it sound like a form of espionage."

"Information is a valuable commodity. Everyone likes to protect their own and get the other guy's."

"Is that what this call is about? Getting the other guy's information."

"I think it's more about checking the reliability of my own. And you are here," he said with undisguised satisfaction. "So far, so good."

Tyler frowned. "What else do you think you know?"

Laurence leaned forward. "You're going to be at the APCU reception tomorrow. That's going to make it quite an event."

"More sources?"

"The guest list is public, Tyler. Easy to check. If you want to." He leaned back and cocked his head in amusement. "Anyway, it'll be good to see you again, whatever the reason."

"Too bad psy perception doesn't work over the phone," Tyler said smoothly. "We might have had a really interesting conversation. But I guess that'll keep until tomorrow. I'll look for you."

Laurence nodded. "By the way," he said, his voice turning somber, "when you see Jonas, tell him, *my* sources say Hardin Toller's been snooping around. I can't say into what."

Tyler cut in quickly. "Can't say or won't say?"

Laurence smiled grimly. "Just tell him, keep an eye out." Then he ended the call.

Tyler sat, staring at the now blank display panel and weighing the implications of what Laurence had said. If he'd needed to confirm his information about her arrival, he could have done that without contacting her, had done so in fact by checking the APCU guest list. As for the vague warning about Toller, that too was hardly necessary. Jonas always kept his eye on that legislator.

So why had Laurence called? Tyler smiled to herself. To tell her, indirectly, he knew she was in metro at Jonas' request. Why he wanted her to know that and how much more he knew, it was impossible to tell. Despite what Laurence had deliberately given away, she couldn't help wondering about things he hadn't let slip, like whether he really had contacts in Psy Management leaking information to him. And whether he knew she and Jonas had met with Chief Wilkins that afternoon. Knowing how Laurence operated, she thought both were a distinct possibility.

Suddenly the impact of suspecting Laurence Meredith in a case of serial murder hit with full force. "Damn it, Jonas," Tyler said aloud. Pushing aside uncomfortable speculations, she tried to concentrate on everything she had learned from Jonas and Wilkins, but finally restlessness overcame her. She decided to see if a walk through the park would help settle her. She locked the reader in the wall safe and set the alarm. She slid her phone out of its slot in the apps pad. She picked up a jacket, put the phone in a pocket, and headed out.

The central entrance of the hotel faced directly across from an ornate gateway set in one of the short sides of the park. A security kiosk stood just inside the gate. The guard nodded as she passed and she gave him a brief wave.

It was still early evening and a few other people were strolling in the park, but not many. Tyler started along a paved walk that ran lengthwise into the park. Half way through, she reached a cross path. At the intersection of the two walks, in a circle of grass, stood a memorial of some kind. A piece of typically nondescript public art unable, Tyler thought, to compete for impressiveness with the stand of trees behind it.

Curious, she walked over to the memorial. In the back of her mind, she had known it was there, but she couldn't remember what it commemorated, if she'd ever known. She read the brass plate and smiled to herself. The uninspired block of granite had been erected to the memory of D. Hollins Riscoll, the legislator who, about twenty years ago, had hammered out the legislative package which still governed the lives of psy perceivers.

Becoming aware of others approaching, Tyler retreated to one of the benches which ringed the monument. She watched as a family group walked up, two adults, two children. The man, who she sorted as husband and father, was consulting his apps pad. "And this monument is carved from genuine granite, one of the few remaining in the city," he read.

The two children ran their fingers over the stone. One of them complained, "It doesn't feel any different."

The woman peered at the inscription and said, "Riscoll. Who's that?"

The man consulted the information on his apps pad again. "Oh, yeah, I remember. He was that pro-psike legislator from a while back." After a few moments, the family, their interest exhausted, moved on.

Staring after them, Tyler reflected how the man had used the derogatory term 'psike' thoughtlessly. It was natural to him and it would be to his kids. The observation did nothing to improve her mood.

She had come out, hoping to distract herself from the concerns of Jonas and the Chief but now she let her thoughts drift back to what they wanted from her. She kept coming back especially to Laurence and Dorian. One was a friend, the other, well, she and Dorian weren't just temperamentally opposite. There seemed to be an automatic antagonism between them. Dorian inevitably irritated her, probably with some deliberation. It was unlikely a high range psy perceiver like Dorian could always manage to say the wrong thing, to needle just a little more than Tyler found comfortable, simply by accident. Especially given Dorian's line of work.

Dorian pursued a lucrative freelance occupation which carried the innocuous title of personnel consultant. Behind the neutral words lay a position of considerable power, for Dorian assisted in search procedures for the major corporates. Tyler had heard Dorian was willing to bend the law a little in her rather delicate and precarious profession. And that her flexibility in such matters had gone a long way to winning for her the preeminent place she held in her field.

It was certainly illegal to require anyone to submit to a hiring interview in the presence of a psy perceiver. Over the years there had been a spate of lawsuits accusing corporates of using personnel procedures that violated privacy rights. Dorian herself had been involved in one of the splashier of these cases. But the people who took their complaints to court, if they won, never seemed to advance beyond the jobs they were awarded by law. Whatever their real feelings on the matter, serious seekers for the highest levels of corporate employment 'voluntarily' accepted the presence of Dorian or someone like her throughout their hiring process. It had become well known in the circles where such knowledge was necessary that an unwillingness to submit to an interview in the presence of a telepath would surely block an applicant from the top ranks of corporate positions.

Because she had played a role in the selection of so many key executives, Dorian was catered to and, certainly to some extent, feared by some of the otherwise most influential people in the country. And it was evident, even on casual acquaintance, that Dorian enjoyed her status and her power. Tyler greatly suspected part of that enjoyment stemmed from Dorian's satisfaction in subjecting the normal population to a taste of the rigorously close personality examinations which were mandated for psy perceivers.

Still whatever bending of the rules Dorian practiced and whatever ego gratification it brought, it all had to be within the bounds of acceptability for her to pass her profiles. Unless, of course, Dorian were that fearsome thing in the minds of conventional perceivers, a psy who could fool the profile examiners, who could generate a psychological profile within the range of normality and yet carry the potential for vastly more anti-social behavior. Not an unusual character in quikvid thrillers, no matter how nonexistent in real life.

Despite the friction between them, Tyler found herself resisting the thought that Dorian could be a mad, marauding murderer. And not simply because the scenario was so unlikely. In fact, Tyler wondered if her rejection of that possibility was not primarily a defense mechanism, a need to prove to herself she was not so petty as to want Dorian to be guilty simply because she didn't like her very much.

As for Jonas' other concern, Laurence Meredith was an entirely different proposition. Although like Dorian it was hard to imagine him in any environment other than a major metro, in almost every other way he was her opposite. Dorian was motivated primarily by the drive for personal power and prestige. Laurence was president and founder of the League for Psy Rights and his whole life was devoted to that cause. Dividing his time between Philly Sector and NY/DC, he lived for his work, his constant lobbying and politicking for the rights of psy perceivers to be treated as ordinary private citizens, with the same legal standing as conventionals.

In his public stances, he never raised issues so inflammatory that they would alienate the mainstream political leaders whose support he needed. He was particularly careful to keep the League's image free from any taint of radicalism. But from private communications, Tyler knew Laurence objected to even the most accepted forms of psy regulation. In fact, he maintained close liaison with some of the most staunch supporters of absolute self-determination for psy perceivers, including those who pushed for abolishing identification by control factor rating. And Tyler suspected that Laurence, like Dorian, would bend the rules for what he considered a good enough reason.

Laurence practiced skillfully the art of separating deeply held belief from public posture. Could it be argued that this trait suggested a personality too adept in duplicity? Could Laurence have mastered the means of deceiving the profile examiners? He certainly had extensively researched the techniques of profile compilation. Tyler suspected he knew them as well as the examiners themselves.

Laurence was a friend, much closer than Dorian. Yet the thought that he might be a murderer did not strike Tyler as impossible.

Abruptly Tyler stood up. "Damn it, Jonas," she said again. She felt like she had been spinning characters for one of her novels. Only Laurence and Dorian weren't characters. They were Jonas and Chief Wilkin's best leads. And despite the Chief's disclaimer about clearing them, what he and Jonas really hoped was that she would be able to turn one of them into the chief suspect. Tyler shook her head.

She walked over to the monument. Like the child before her, she ran her fingers over the stone. The kid was right. You couldn't tell it from synthetic.

If anything, more disheartened than she had been when she set out, Tyler walked back to the hotel and the promise of a restless night.

The next morning, Tyler woke feeling heavy and groggy. She had tossed and turned for the first part of the night and then ended up sleeping later than she had expected. Still she stalled before leaving for Jonas' office. Aside from telling him about Laurence's call, there didn't seem to be much to do except wait for the evening and the APCU reception. The entire day stretched bleakly toward that end and Tyler was in no particular hurry to get there.

She nursed a cup of coffee and thought some more about Laurence. She wondered if a large part of his intent in calling her had been to serve notice on Jonas that his turf was not quite as much under his control as he might like to think. She wondered even more if Laurence had any idea that he himself was part of Jonas' worries. That, at least, she'd probably find out tonight.

Seeking distraction, Tyler turned on the vid and found herself staring into the ever cheerful face of Doug Selnik, PsyCF3. It was a talk show and Doug was hyping his new book, his most recent effort to explain psy perception to a mass market. She had read it in draft form and hadn't liked it. But then she didn't care for any of his books. They were as unrelentingly, even aggressively, cheerful as

Doug was. Still his stuff was popular and so was Doug's image. Psy perceiver as friendly puppy dog. All it did was bring Tyler's thoughts back to the reception. Doug Selnik would almost certainly be there. One more thing not to look forward to.

Excerpts from a draft for *Getting Wise to Psy: An Informal Introduction to Psy Perception* by Dr. Douglas Selnik, PhD, PsyCF3

In the previous chapter, we've cleared up a couple of misconceptions about psy perception. First of all it doesn't operate over long distances. Remember, the range of its various functions (sorting, screening, even impartment) is roughly equivalent to the distance the human voice can carry. Second, for the most part psy perception doesn't pass through solid surfaces. So we can stop worrying about somebody sorting what's going on across town. Or next door for that matter, unless you've left the doors and windows open.

Let's move on now to another common misunderstanding about psy perception. Many people believe it provides a good means for normal communication. In other words, they think a little silent psy perceiving beats out old fashioned conversation every time.

Well, it just ain't so.

Now, I know you're going to say what all my normally perceiving friends say. Gimme a break, Doc. It's got to be a lot easier to share thoughts than to talk to each other.

Of course, what you'd be missing is that before you can communicate much of anything to anyone, you've got to find a way to organize it. For most of us that means putting it into words. Oh, sure, we humans can communicate in nonverbal ways. We have grunts and groans, gestures and expressions. But all of that's pretty general. We might refer to those nonverbal means of communication as 'primal.' At least, that's what a lot of my colleagues like to call it.

And a raised eyebrow or a raised fist can tell us a fair amount about what another person is feeling. But you just can't beat putting things into words for getting into the details of communication. By the way, my colleagues have taken to calling verbal communication 'formal' because each language is really a separate set of forms or customs we have to learn.

Now when it comes to psy perception, we have to realize that no one, not even a CF4 (just in case you happen to know one), can perceive what isn't there. That means anything you actually intend to communicate usually has to be put into words for psy perceivers just like for anyone else.

So, let's imagine you're having a conversation with a psy friend. And you're going to save yourself the trouble of talking. All you've got to do is think out what you want to say and, presto, your friend will be able to sort everything even though you haven't actually said a word.

Well, try it sometime. What you'll find is that it's darn awkward to form sentences in your head without actually saying the words. Oh, sure, one or two is not a problem. But the farther you go in your conversation, the more you lose track of what you're trying to say just because you don't actually have to say it. Pretty soon your thoughts are running off in all different directions. By then your psy perceiving friend is going to have a pretty glazed look on his or her face trying to keep up with you.

There have been some interesting studies done on the relationship between formal communication, remember that means verbal or with words, and the actual formation or articulation of those words. I have included a couple of references at the end of this chapter for those of you who are brave enough to tackle the so-called professional articles. But I can summarize a lot of the scientific jargon for you. The studies show that it's awfully hard to figure out what you mean until you say it. And it's a lot easier to say things out loud than to try to keep track of thinking them out in your head. And by the way, that seems to be true even for people with the highest ranges of psy ability. I know it's true for me. That's why, generally, psy perceivers talk as much as anybody else. And make about as much sense, or as little, as the case may be.

OK. I can hear your 'yeah, but' right now. And that 'yeah, but' is saying that psy perceivers pick up a lot that's unsaid. Well, I'm not going to argue with that because that's exactly what psy perception mostly does pick up, the things that aren't said, or at least aren't said very clearly. All that stuff that's buzzing around in us when we aren't trying to think of or say anything in particular. Things we notice, bits and pieces of words and phrases, general mood, even images that sometimes form in our minds, all those things that we have come to call the 'constant.' Actually many of my colleagues prefer 'undifferentiated aware state,' but I think that's a bit of mouthful, don't you?

And what tends to happen when you're not actually talking to someone, or writing as I am to you, is that the constant takes over. Oh, there's plenty of stuff there all right, but nobody's bothered to make any sense out of it. And believe me, that's no easy task. In fact, if you remember from our earlier discussion, that's exactly one of the points that separates different levels of psy capability. The higher the psy rating the easier it is to select something out of the constant that actually means anything. Or at least, that the psy perceiver *thinks* means anything. Because there's always room for interpretation. You have a random thought or an image. Is that something you know or actually experienced? Or is it something you're worried about, or wishing for? Those things aren't always clear.

And I guess that brings us to my last point about why psy perceivers aren't about to give up normal conversation. Even if two psy perceivers decide to 'think' their sentences at each other, they have to deal not only with all that random background noise in the constant but also with the differences in sorting ability across the control factor ratings, and even the considerable variation in that ability among those with the same rating.

Let me see if I can give you an example of what I mean. Let's imagine we were trying to communicate with music instead of words. Let's suppose we have one person who can hear every nuance of a complicated musical composition. This person hears phrasing, changes of tempo, harmonic patterns, all the elements. Then we have another person who can hear the music but pretty much just hears the melody, just hears what's going through the ear at the moment. Finally we have someone who hears the music, all right, but is tone deaf.

Now that's what it might be like trying to communicate relying only on psy perception. You're never going to have the three people in my example hearing music the same way. And you're not likely to have two or three psy perceivers so well matched in what they 'hear" by sorting that they will efficiently 'talk' without ever feeling the need to resort to speech.

Let's review our two basic points. Number one, it's a lot easier to speak words than to think them. And two, given the variations in psy capability, that's as true for psy perceivers as it is for our normally perceiving friends. That's why, psy perception or no, good old-fashioned conversation is going to be with us for a long, long time.

Email from Laurence Meredith to Tyler West: Tyler, if you can find a spare moment, try to take a look at the enclosed material. It's Doug's usual stuff. Too cutesy precious we're all just folks together for my taste but it seems to get the job done. He's probably overstated (a little) the difficulties of unspoken communication, particularly between high level psy perceivers. I think the reliance on speech, at some levels anyway, is mostly habit and a desire not to be too conspicuous. But he's close enough for the audience he's trying to reach. I'm not sure his music analogy really delivers. Any thoughts? Laurence

Email from Tyler West to Laurence Meredith: Yes. Tell Doug to turn in his word processor and go back to his lab. Oh, well, his stuff does sell. The static of radio transmission and the noise of vid transmission seem to me better metaphors than music to get across the concept he's working with. The formless aware-state data of the constant might be likened to static interfering with organized non-vocalization. I like that better than the video noise comparison. I'm not sure why but it seems easier to relate psy perception to hearing than to seeing, which seems to have occurred to Doug as well. He's more right than you are about the problems of using psy perception for extended unspoken communication. Your ability to 'screen the static' is considerably above average. Should I subtract the fee for editorial consultation from my annual subscription to the League, or do you want me to bill you directly? Tyler

Email from Laurence Meredith to Tyler West: Very funny. Mess around with your annual donation and I'll have Doug mention your name as 'one of those who made this book possible.' Anyway he thought the static idea was OK, just a little too mechanical. (His word, not mine.) I think he's going to use both comparisons, music and radio transmission. It's been a long time. Do you ever leave that sylvan glade of yours? That's literary talk. Laurence

Chapter Eight

By midmorning Tyler gave up on trying to distance herself from the main focus of the day. She headed for Psy Management. When she arrived Cal intercepted her outside Jonas' office with the news that Hardin Toller had come barging in about half an hour ago.

"He's in with him now," he said, nodding toward Jonas' door. Tyler could tell the brief encounter with Toller was still with Cal, like a bad taste. Also that he had sorted nothing useful when Toller had stormed through demanding to see Jonas. "Probably a coincidence his showing up today," Cal added. He was trying to reassure himself. "There's no reason he should be onto anything."

"That's not what Laurence said," Tyler retorted. She proceeded to tell Cal about last night's phone call.

Cal shrugged. "That still doesn't mean Toller has anything specific. He's always stirring things up. Laurence knows that."

"That's what I told myself," Tyler said discontentedly. "Be nice if I were convinced." Frowning, she stared at the blank door to Jonas' office. "Only I'm not."

Hardin Toller, federal legislator for NorEast Philly Sector, District 32, had the kind of personality often attributed to small men. Everything in life put him on the defensive. Nothing was neutral, everything was threatening. He compensated for his defensiveness by constantly maintaining a posture of attack. Even in conversation, the remarks of others were enemy volleys to be heeded only as necessary to counter them. For Toller, life was a combat zone in which every interaction that was not a clear victory was a certain defeat. And in his ceaseless war, he had long ago identified his worst enemies.

He hated psy perceivers. He hated them for having weapons which had been denied him, and worse, weapons whose power he could not accurately gauge. No matter how cleverly he attacked or counterattacked, he was sure a psike could always slip behind his lines. He found that intolerable.

And yet Toller was not a small man, at least not physically. He was heavy but no one looking at him would ever think of him as fat. At just over six feet, he was tall, but he was also broad, giving the impression more of massiveness than of height. Even seated, as he was now before Jonas' desk, his presence seemed to crowd the room.

The two men waited, Jonas outwardly impassive, Toller, his face set in unalterable lines of stubborn purpose.

At last when the silence between them had stretched long enough to establish that Jonas would not open the conversation, Toller abruptly said, "You're fucking around with something, Acre, and you're going to tell me what it is."

Jonas kept still, for the moment ignoring the insult. Then he gave a slight dismissive nod. "This agency conducts a considerable range of public business, Legislator. And we keep public records. To those, you, and any other citizen, are welcome. I'll call a clerk." Jonas reached for his apps pad.

Toller slammed a hand down on the desk. "Don't give me that high ass bureaucrat act. *You* talk to me."

Jonas pointedly glanced at the time display. "Unfortunately my entire day is scheduled."

"You make time for me, Acre." Toller put offense into every word.

"Perhaps if you'd tell me what this is about, Legislator." Jonas assumed the tone of a harried administrator trying to extend courtesy under difficult circumstances. Inwardly he very much wanted to find out just what lay behind Toller's fishing expedition.

As nastily as he could Toller said, "No, Commissioner, you tell me."

An expression which Jonas could not quite read came over Toller's face. Whatever had brought Toller, Jonas was pretty sure he didn't actually expect to get any information. What he was after was Jonas' reaction. Sometimes you revealed almost as much by the way you concealed information as by giving it.

Jonas decided it was time to allow himself a little anger. "Look, Toller, you come barging in here with riddles and insults. I don't have time for it. If there's something on your mind, say it. If not..." Jonas stared coldly at Toller.

A heavy silence dragged between them again. At last Toller seemed to decide Jonas wasn't going to respond without something specific to goad him. "The day before yesterday you drove north to see that reclusive freak West. Yesterday she turned up in metro and you both met with Wilkins." Clearly Toller considered he had made his challenge.

Jonas sat impassively, trying to mask his surprise. He hoped he managed it. He also inwardly cursed himself for getting into this situation, but now the problem was how to handle it. It was clear Toller knew enough for denial to be pointless, and probably dangerous. It would only convince Toller there was something to hide.

At last Jonas said, "Yes, Tyler West and I met with Chief Wilkins yesterday." His voice conveyed surprise over Toller's interest in such trivia. At least, he hoped it did. "On matters of liaison between Psy Management and Enforcement, if you want to know."

"You have a public record of this meeting, I assume," Toller sneered.

"It was an informal, private meeting, Legislator."

"Bull shit."

"That's enough, Toller." This time there was nothing calculated in Jonas' anger.

"No, Commissioner, not anywhere near enough." Toller stood up, allowing his considerable bulk to loom over Jonas' desk. "Listen, Acre, I know how you operate. You've got your pet psikes, like West, trained to jump when you say. When you want to poke into something, and you don't want anybody to know about it. Then there's no Demand. When there's no Demand, there's no public record. No accountability. But you better hear me, you're not going to get away with it this time. Not with the public safety at stake. I'll see to it. If you and Wilkins abridge the Internal Security Act, I'll hang you out to dry. The both of you."

Toller ended the interview as abruptly as he had started it. He was up and out the door before Jonas could react. On his way out he all but ran headlong into Tyler and Cal who were waiting in the anteroom to Jonas' office.

The three of them confronted each other for a moment in silence. Toller's emotions washed over the two psy like an acid bath. Then he shouldered his way past them.

Tyler and Cal walked through into Jonas' office where he still sat, relatively expressionless. But, as they easily sorted, he churned with anger and frustration. "Shit," he said quietly, but emphatically.

Tyler sat in the chair which Toller had just vacated. "Among other things," she said, "I came to give you a warning." Her lips curved upward to a minimal smile. "A warning from Laurence. He said to tell you, watch out for Hardin Toller."

Jonas responded first to her tone. "Thanks," he said with appropriate sarcasm. But then his attention focused. "When did you talk to Laurence?"

"He called last night."

"He called you here in metro? At your hotel?" Jonas was genuinely surprised. "How did he know where you were staying?"

He hadn't actually expected an answer to the last question, but Tyler said, "He told me he had his sources. He said he was confirming their accuracy."

"You believe that?"

"I believe it, as far as it goes. But he must also have wanted to let me know, to let us know, he knew you called me in."

"Hmmm...is that all he said?"

"Pretty much, except for the warning about Toller. Which I've obviously delivered a little late."

"Toller," Jonas spit out the name. "He knows I went to see you." He looked at Tyler. "He knows we met with Chief Wilkins yesterday. He threatened me with public safety and the ISA." Tyler and Cal exchanged glances. With a rueful grimace, Jonas said, "Didn't need to say any of that, did I?"

Cal shrugged. "That's all pretty much on the surface of your constant," he said. "But it seems like Toller didn't connect with anything specific. No mention of murder or anything?"

Jonas shook his head. "I think he's just fishing. If he had anything substantive, he wouldn't have come to me. It'd be a press conference announcing the convening of a legislative hearing. A well-publicized legislative hearing."

"He knows something. He's just not sure what." It was Tyler who spoke and they both looked at her. "I'm not certain. He didn't give me much time. But I think he's had some kind of communication. Probably anonymous."

Jonas was pleased at what Tyler had sorted, Cal was impressed. "Any idea about details?" Cal asked.

"No," she said. "I'd really be guessing on that."

"But your hunch is, it's this business."

"I'd say, it's more than a hunch."

A burst of frustration erupted from Jonas. "Just great," he said. "This has got to be kept quiet and Toller's already nosing around. How could he know anything? Unless there's a leak at Enforcement."

Tyler shook her head. "I don't think so. His knowledge...he's not really sure how reliable it is. Not sure he can trust his source."

"Well, between Laurence and Toller, something's got out on the grape vine," Cal said.

Jonas' attention switched abruptly. "Laurence. Laurence, too," he said as if he had forgotten. "Damn it. What in the hell do they know?"

The question was rhetorical but Cal decided to answer it. "They both know you've got Tyler here for something. Something you don't want to make official, something important you don't want generally known." He looked at Tyler for confirmation, then added.

"Fortunately neither one of them realizes just what it is we're investigating. Not yet anyway," he concluded glumly.

Tyler nodded. "Whatever Toller's got, Jonas is right. It's not enough to go public with. Or he would. As for Laurence, that'll have to wait till tonight."

"I hope you can turn up something," Jonas said to her. "Meanwhile we'll warn the Chief about Toller. He's bound to turn up at Enforcement soon."

As for Toller, most of their conclusions were correct. He himself wasn't exactly sure what he knew. All he had was an anonymous email. His staff had traced its source. It was one of thousands which had been sent that day through a server at a chat café, with no record of who had written it. Probably just a crank. Toller got these kinds of things all the time. But he never dismissed any of them out of hand. He had his staff sift through them all. And he had an instinct about this one, that here was something he could use. The interview with Acre tended to weigh in favor of that feeling.

The email read: "Legislator Toller: In the interests of public safety, here are some questions that need answers. Why has Jonas Acre brought Tyler West, PsyCF4, into metro? Why are Acre and West meeting secretly with Wilkins of Enforcement? What is it they're trying to keep out of the public record? Clever bureaucrats bend the law to suit themselves. Only someone with your position and authority can see to it that the public interest is protected. A concerned citizen."

It hadn't taken much checking to find out West had turned up in metro after a visit from Acre, and that they had both met with Wilkins, if not secretly, at least very quietly. And whatever was behind West's arrival and the meeting with Wilkins, it was important enough to lie about. Acre hadn't been stupid enough to deny the meeting outright, but T. West sure hadn't dragged her ass into metro for a PR meeting.

Whatever was going on, Toller insisted to himself, he'd give Acre and West his full attention. Whatever they were after, he'd force it out into the open soon enough.

Chapter Nine

Jonas had arranged a ceevee to take Tyler to the civic center. She arrived at the APCU reception in time to join the first wave of early arrivals. The main entry to the impressive rectangular room in which the reception was being held led down a gently angled flight of broad stairs on one of the shorter walls. Directly across the room was another stairway. Connecting the two stairways at the entrance level was a mezzanine which encircled the room below. There were service doors off the main room itself, but they blended discreetly with the walls into which they were set.

Instead of immediately descending the nearer stairs, Tyler turned to her right and walked halfway along the railing of the mezzanine. There she stopped and looked down at the scene below. A fair sized crowd had already congregated around the buffet table which ran almost the length of the room. A great incoherent babble of mental activity rose to her, the psyonic equivalent of the generalized sound of the spoken conversations which also drifted up. She concentrated briefly on both sets of noise and then redirected her attention to more specific purposes.

She was looking for either Laurence or Dorian. However, she doubted that Dorian had yet arrived, a late entrance being more to her taste. But she spotted Laurence without much difficulty. He stood near the base of the farther stairway. He held a plate in one hand. With the other, he gestured in emphatic conversation with someone she didn't know.

After a short time, Laurence lightly tapped the arm of the man he was speaking with and then moved away. Tyler watched as he spoke another word here and there, put down his plate, and then wandered up the stairs. All the seemingly normal random activity of just such a social gathering. But she knew as she watched him that he had noticed her and was deliberately on his way.

As Laurence walked casually along the mezzanine, he continued to stop and exchange a few words with other people who were also enjoying the vantage point provided by the balcony. He smiled frequently, the light brown of his face warm with what appeared to be genuine pleasure at greeting those he met. When he finally arrived to within a few steps of where Tyler was standing, he gave a very natural impression of noticing her for the first time.

Aloud, he said, "Well, Tyler, it is you. I saw your name on the list but could hardly believe you'd actually turn up." He joined her at the railing. "How long has it been?" Underlying his words was a dominant mix of humor and curiosity. And now standing beside her, he articulated in his mind, how's my performance?

With equal precision, Tyler silently formed the words, just what I would expect from a good politician.

Laurence turned to face her and said aloud, "Good politicians also need to be well informed." He glanced around, but they were virtually alone despite the crowd below and the few milling clusters of people along the mezzanine. "You are here because of Jonas, aren't you?"

"I thought you established that on the phone last night."

"Did you give him my message?"

Tyler didn't answer immediately but continued to look down at the increasingly crowded room below them. The dominant impression she got from Laurence was still curiosity, but now joined by concern.

"Yes," she finally said. "Unfortunately by the time I delivered it, Toller was already storming out of his office."

Laurence reacted with more concern, but with anger too. "That man is dangerous. If one of us had a psychological profile like his, they'd lock us up." He let the flare up within him subside. "What did Toller want?"

Tyler turned to face him. "Something similar to what you want, I think." Laurence stiffened. "By dangling a hint of knowing something, to see if he could learn more."

Physically Laurence relaxed, but he was screening very carefully. "You will, I hope, grant a difference in our motives."

"Yes, I'll give you that. Now, tell me, just what do you know?"

Laurence shrugged but his outer casualness was still at odds with his inner wariness. "Pretty much what I told you. I know Jonas has got you down here poking into something. That Toller has somehow been alerted. And whatever it is, it's got Jonas by the..." He formed a brief, graphic image. Tyler smiled wryly. "Anyway that's about it." He looked at her with dark intent eyes. "I don't suppose you'd tell me what it's all about?"

Tyler returned Laurence's stare, her own expression a combination of humor and challenge. "I don't suppose you'd tell me how you know? That there's anything to inquire about, I mean."

"It seems to me, I've already told you more than you've told me."

"Only because you have ulterior motives, Laurence."

"Look who's talking."

A sudden commotion at the head of the main stairway broke in upon them. They both turned and watched the arrival of Dorian Rath. As usual, Dorian arrived with a retinue. Standing immediately next to her and obviously in the role of escort was a strikingly handsome man, who even Tyler recognized as a cine actor of ascendent reputation.

Dorian's party also included a highly regarded traditional media artist, a well-known composer of synthesized music, a lawyer who specialized in psyonics and her husband, and two prominent corporate execs with their spouses.

As always, Dorian herself was, if not flamboyant, certainly commanding of attention. She was dressed in a flowing robe made of an iridescent material which shimmered between deep purple and deep green. Tyler reflected she had never seen a color like it except on the head of a mallard drake. As that image floated through her mind, she heard a muffled grunt of amusement from Laurence. Above that exotic color, Dorian's short white-blonde hair seemed to be alight from within. It gleamed like the chain of silver links she wore around her neck. Suspended from the chain was a large trident-shaped pendant, the Greek letter *psi*.

As Dorian stood momentarily at the head of the stairs, there was a perceptible drop in the noise level, both psy and non-psy. With impeccable timing, Dorian caught the brief lull and, without seeming to raise her voice yet with sufficient projection to reach even where Laurence and Tyler stood, said, "Let the revels begin."

Laurence, with a sourness of voice that matched his feeling, muttered, "Let them begin indeed, since the court jester has arrived."

"That hardly sounds like a politician," Tyler said.

"You're no great fan of Dorian, so I can afford a very unpolitical honesty."

"Style notwithstanding, Dorian's too smart to be anyone's jester."

"She's too fond of self-dramatization for my taste. And for yours, too, whether you're in the mood to admit it." Laurence let his gaze wander back to the stairs which Dorian and her party were now descending. Tyler could almost hear the counters clicking in his head. "Dorian is the only other CF4 here tonight," he said. "Besides us, I mean." Laurence looked at Tyler reflectively. "But you already knew that, didn't you? And you wouldn't be here except for Jonas." He glanced back at Dorian. "Well, that's got to be part of it. Jonas wanted you to see both of us. That *is* right, isn't it?"

Tyler ignored the question. "Tell me something, Laurence. Would you consent to a full scale examination, unofficially? If the reason were good enough."

Laurence's face darkened. Inwardly he flared with sudden anger which he made no attempt to screen. "Of course not. You know better than that."

Tyler turned and considered him very seriously. "Not even to avert a major disaster?"

He shook his head, but not in answer to her question. Instead it was a gesture of frustration. "Sometimes I think you really don't understand. The reasons a government gives for overriding the individual always sound convincing. It's always national security and the general welfare. And in the end, there is no security, and there is no general welfare. Not where it counts. In the real lives of individual people." Laurence's passion was genuine, the practiced rhythms of his words notwithstanding. He continued with the same fervor. "I'll tell you something, Tyler. You should tell me what this is all about. I'll find out eventually. Maybe then it'll be too late. For now, tell Jonas, if he wants anything from me, he's going to have to make it official. Let him call a Demand on me. Let him know that all of us are not quite so accommodating as you."

Chapter Ten

After Laurence left her, Tyler wandered off and made her way down to the main floor. She hadn't learned much from him, but then she hadn't expected to. She was sure he knew more than he had admitted, but exactly what it was she couldn't determine. As for what he had learned from her, he had made the connection about himself and Dorian being the focus of her attention, but that he had figured out, not sorted. And as far as she could tell, he didn't seem to have any idea about the series of deaths Jonas was worried about. At least she had learned why he had approached her in the first place. He wanted information from her. He hoped, by revealing that he already knew something, to make her more willing to provide it.

The evening began to flow with the rhythm peculiar to all such gatherings. It passed in a stream of small talk broken by almost ritualized movements from person to person, group to group. Tyler grew weary of variations on, "What a surprise to see you here. How long has it been?" The rest of her conversations did not seem to progress beyond, "Read your latest. Working on anything new?"

At one point, Cal Houlston came by to see how everything was going, but he didn't stay. He felt he needed to keep close to Jonas. A little later, Doug Selnik stopped her to deliver lavish praise of her last book. Also to thank her with unnecessary enthusiasm for her helpful comments on his own. "Laurence told me he'd sent you a draft copy. I wouldn't have thought of imposing myself, you understand."

Tyler listened to his chatter until she could politely excuse herself. Through all the progression of small talk, the greater part of

Tyler's attention was directed at Dorian who continued always to be at the center of a small group that consisted of the party she had arrived with, plus a varying crew of additions. It would be easy to drift into the cluster of people around Dorian, but unlikely to have a chance to get her alone in private conversation without making an issue of it. Nevertheless Tyler had just decided to introduce herself to the outer perimeter of Dorian's circle when someone lightly touched her arm. She turned and found herself face to face with Jonas' wife.

"You are Tyler West, aren't you? I believe we met once. At Jonas' investiture as commissioner. I'm Meryl Acre. His wife."

The words had been neutral and the voice poised, but it was clear to Tyler that M. Acre was extremely anxious. Somewhat feebly, Tyler said, "Yes, it's nice to see you again."

"Oh, I guess you don't really remember me." Meryl Acre looked around the room, her nervousness rising. "I shouldn't do this, I know, but..." She looked around again.

"I think Jonas is upstairs." Tyler responded automatically to Meryl Acre's unease. "No need to be concerned about him."

Meryl Acre's mouth twitched. "I guess special talents do come in handy."

Tyler let the remark pass. "What is it you wanted?" she asked.

"You're here tonight...well, Jonas arranged for you to be here, didn't he?" Before Tyler could frame a polite and lying denial, Meryl Acre hurried on, "I know you won't answer that. It's just whatever it is...the reason Jonas wanted you to be here. I've never seen him like this, he's always so calm. It's something really serious, isn't it?"

Tyler felt moved to sudden sympathy for Jonas' wife. Her worry was so strong and evident. But all Tyler said was, "I'm sorry. I can't...There's nothing I can tell you."

"Yes, there's one thing. Just one thing. Is Jonas putting himself in danger? Just tell me that?"

Tyler hesitated. It was obvious Meryl Acre was convinced something had Jonas deeply disturbed. Answering that question as honestly as possible wasn't going to reveal anything Meryl Acre hadn't already decided was true. So Tyler finally said, "I'm not sure I know, but I don't believe he is. What he's worried about. It's not personal danger. His concern is on a somewhat larger scale."

Meryl Acre seemed to be weighing Tyler's truthfulness. "It's something to do with you...with psy perceivers, isn't it?"

"That is Jonas' work."

"Yes. I wish it weren't." The bitterness in Meryl Acre was strong. "I don't mean anything against you...you people. But I wish he'd resign." She turned and walked away before Tyler could reply, which was just as well because Tyler had no reply to give.

The encounter left Tyler unsettled. Meryl Acre's concern for her husband was understandable, but that concern had evidently provoked in her a deep antipathy to his work. And it was clear, Jonas didn't know how his wife felt. If he did, Tyler knew she would have sorted it from him. It seemed strange to her that two people could be so close and not pick up at least the external signals of such deep discomfort. But then again, Jonas was completely caught up in what he saw as a looming crisis. He had little attention to spare.

As for Meryl Acre herself, she was frightened only for him, rather than having to share the more cataclysmic vision which obsessed him. Although if it came to it, Meryl Acre would probably rather contemplate an anti-psy riot than the death of her husband.

Tyler had fallen into such a state of abstraction that for a few minutes she was literally unaware of everything around her. But her preoccupation was abruptly broken by a well modulated but commanding voice. "Fancy seeing you here. How long has it been?" With a careful placement of stress Dorian Rath mimicked the phrases Tyler had been hearing all evening. It seemed as if the problem of joining Dorian's circle had been solved for her. Dorian turned back to address the people around her. "I don't think any of you know Tyler West, not her personally, although her books, of course."

So introductions were made and everyone except the artist made polite noises about Tyler's work. He said, "I never read novels."

Dorian laughed. "I think I shall commence never to look at paintings." Her tone was teasing and there was mockery in her acid green eyes. "And I warn you, Seth, Tyler is more truly an artist than you. You earn your bread with your daubing. Tyler is independently wealthy and writes for the love of it."

One of the executives, whose name was Tasa Weldon, made the connection. "Are you one of *the* West's?"

"My grandfather was Harold West, so I suppose I am." Tyler didn't bother to hide her irritation.

Dorian cut in, still with a mocking note in her voice. "And since I so rarely get to hobnob with old money, you will excuse us for a moment." And she walked off to the side of the room, expecting Tyler to follow, which she did.

There were tables along the wall, well out of the crowd. When they were seated at one, Dorian said, "I don't know why you're so touchy. They were very impressed."

"Somehow I hardly think you need me to impress your friends."

"Not friends, surely, except for Ivor. He may be an actor but even you'd like him. Anyway a little aggravation is a small price to pay for getting what you want." Dorian felt very self-satisfied and did nothing to mask her feeling. When Tyler didn't respond, Dorian continued, "You did want to talk to me alone, didn't you? I've had more than a distinct impression of that all evening."

"And all along, I thought I was being rather subtle."

"Perhaps it's not your lack of subtlety, but rather the acuity of my perception," Dorian said with teasing formality. Then, more naturally, she added. "My way, both of us get credit. Which we certainly seem to deserve. After all, with the exception of..." Dorian let her gaze wander around the room as if she needed to remind herself when in fact the name was in her mind all along. "Of Laurence, we are the only CF4s here." She turned back and gave Tyler a very direct stare. "Now, Laurence is here because politicking is his passion. And I'm here because...well, because I never miss an event. The question remains, why are you here? Surely the country mouse didn't venture out just to arrange a conversation with me." A sharpness, an intensity came over Dorian. "Or is that just close enough to the truth?"

Tyler met Dorian's gaze with equal directness. "I'm here in part because I wanted to talk to you, yes."

"If it comes to that, I'm doing most of the talking," Dorian said. "But perhaps that's quite satisfactory."

"You usually do most of the talking, Dorian."

"I am, to say the least, somewhat more gregarious than you, Tyler. But in this case, I suspect this conversation is taking place merely to create an opportunity."

Dorian fell silent and then it was as if whatever social defenses she would normally use were removed. She simply stopped screening her own reactions. A full range of emotional response flowed from her. The first thing Tyler sorted was that Dorian was genuinely curious about what Tyler wanted. But there was also amusement, with herself, with Tyler, with the setting in which they found themselves. Clearly it came to Tyler that Dorian's amusement was that of someone participating in the evening's events mainly for the pleasure of indulging in detached observation. But strongest of all, there was also a sense of challenge and of delight in that challenge. The challenge of a game, a sport, of being able to take a risk and still maintain control.

Dorian's openness lasted less than a minute, and then she re-established normal screening. "So, at least, I have been frank with you," she said. "Far more than you have with me. Or will be." Momentarily, Dorian's inflection had become severe. But she immediately dropped back into her earlier bantering tone. "Have you found out...anything...you wanted to know?"

Tyler paused before answering, trying to choose what to focus on. "You like testing limits, your own and others."

Dorian laughed. "Very good." Then with what seemed to be complete seriousness, she said, "Yes, I am a game player. You write novels where you have total control. I like to live the plot. The level of predictability is so much less." Dorian leaned forward. "Just to have my own little bit out of this conversation, let me say, you're worried about something, country mouse. Very worried." She sat back and looked around the room until she sighted Jonas. "The kind of worries that the commissioner can bring to...such as us. And speaking of worries, and our esteemed commissioner, if it were anyone but Jonas, I'd use the word 'distraught' to describe him. Maybe I'll use it anyway." She glanced back at Tyler. "It'd be an interesting challenge to figure out exactly what's bothering you and Jonas. Beyond, of course," her gaze sharpened again, "the obvious fact that it's got something to do with impartment." She waited. Tyler stared back at her blankly. With a wry smile, Dorian added, "Not exactly sure what. Not yet anyway." Dorian stood up. Her white-blonde head loomed above Tyler like some arrogant star. "There's an old saying about a fair exchange being no robbery. I hope you're satisfied with your end of the bargain."

Dorian walked away. Tyler watched her as she threaded her way through the groups of people who stood chattering around the room. Then someone Tyler remembered having been introduced to came by with some idle remarks about the success of the evening. Someone else stopped to say how much they were looking forward to her next book. The next half hour passed in a parade of similar, meaningless chitchat.

When there was finally a lull, Tyler once again looked over the room. Although it was getting late enough for the crowd to have thinned, she could not spot Laurence or Dorian. She wondered if they had left. And at that point she didn't much care. She was tired, but even more frustrated. The whole evening seemed to have been an exercise in futility.

Chapter Eleven

Willis Crayton hummed softly to himself. That way if he ran into one of them, he'd be protected. They'd hear what he was singing and wouldn't be able to grab his thoughts. It wasn't right having...what should he call them? Not people. Things...beings. Yes, that was it. Like in the quikvids...beings like that free to take over a man's mind whenever they wanted.

What about privacy? A man's thoughts are his own. Should be his own. But not with them around.

Crayton was working in a service corridor which ran behind one of the long walls of the APCU reception room. It was quiet. Not even a rumble of conversation came through the wall. Somewhere at the far end of the hall, he thought he had heard a faint scrape and a click. Maybe someone coming into the corridor at that end. He finished dumping the trash he had collected into the disposal chute and then waited to see if anyone came by. But no one did. Now he was having a smoke before sweeping up. You weren't supposed to smoke, but the supervisor wasn't likely to be checking back here. Too much to keep him busy out front right now. Always break the rules when the boss' eyes are somewhere else.

Like now, the super out there making sure everything was right for those damn psikes. He hadn't dared turn down this job. It woulda been, why don't you want to work that assignment, Mr. Crayton? Are you uncomfortable around psy perceivers? We certainly wouldn't want to put you in a situation which you found disturbing. We'll just mark your file, prefers to avoid psy contact. Prefers to avoid psy contact. Shit. May as well say, don't call Willis Crayton for work. Work contractors didn't like complications. No, bad enough one of those psikes could find out what you thought about them at any time. Come up behind you and read your mind.

Willis Crayton glanced nervously up and down the corridor. Its dim silence was comforting. No. Wouldn't catch any of them back here. Wouldn't catch one of them sweeping floors, picking up garbage.

Containment, that's what was needed. They should all be put off somewhere, somewhere they'd be watched for a change. See how they like it.

A vivid image formed in Willis Crayton's mind. In the background a strong wired enclosure. Within it, gaunt faced people, dressed in shapeless, anonymous clothing, huddled in abject submission. In front, secure in shining uniformed dignity, a strong man, a brave man, a man chosen to stand watch. Willis Crayton knew he could be that man, the guardian, keep them where they belonged. Where they could be no threat.

The image held clear and then broke. It would never happen. They had all the breaks. They knew things no one else could know. Even the government people were afraid of them. Probably had half the politicians blackmailed.

Never happen that is unless someday, somebody rose up and did something. Somebody. Ordinary citizens with guts. They're the only ones who would ever do anything. And then the time would come. Put all those psikes in camps where they belonged. Terminate those who wouldn't cooperate. That's what they had said at the meeting. Those were people who knew how to get things done.

The few must go down before the needs of the many. Besides psikes weren't human really. Just freaks caused by too much radiation in the atmosphere. Who knows, maybe all of them would have to go. Contain 'em or kill 'em. That was the way all right. Be another meeting soon. Had to be. He'd help again. That Bren knew how to get the message across. Contain 'em or kill 'em. Well, he said it better than that. Yeah, Bren was a man who could deliver. Worth helping him. Proud of it. Contain 'em or kill 'em.

What d'ya get if you cross a telepath with a live wire? Fried psy. That's a good one. Fried psy.

God, I hate them, hate them, hate them.

Willis Crayton stood motionless, one hand poised to bring the cigarette to his lips, but now for him there was only his own deeply felt emotion pounding within him, echoing upon itself. For one last faint moment Willis Crayton was aware it was time to stop thinking about psikes and the next meeting, to take a last drag on his cigarette, and get on with his work. But the moment died and the hatred he felt was no longer part of himself. It had become the only self he had.

Fried psy, fried psy, fried psy. Hatethem hatethem hatethem.

No more corridor, no more cigarette, no more Willis Crayton. Only Willis Crayton's hatred. A living entity...a being...that left no room for any other life. What for Willis Crayton had become all time and all space would have been to a more objective observer a couple of minutes. Minutes in which the heart of Willis Crayton pumped frantically to nourish that all encompassing hatred, pumped harder and faster, harder and faster, until the blood vessels feeding his brain burst. Then his heart needed to pump no longer. Willis Crayton, and the hatred he had become, died.

Chapter Twelve

Tyler noticed Cal immediately, but only because she was still sitting at the table where Dorian had left her. Cal appeared at one of the doors set in the side wall. He was obviously coming from the service corridor. She was surprised because he hadn't been far from Jonas all evening, as far as she knew. If she had not been a psy perceiver, she would have reacted first to his face, gone hard edged with shock. But being psy, instead she took in the emotional intensity he projected, a mixture of anguish, anger, and disbelief.

She was at the door in an instant and all but pushed him back out of the room. He stumbled through the door, and Tyler let it shut behind them. Facing him in the dimly lit corridor, she already knew what he had to tell.

"Down there. It's one of the maintenance crew," Cal said shakily. He nodded slightly to his left. Tyler looked down the length of the corridor. At the end of it, someone from building security was standing. Just a few feet in front of him lay what looked like a pile of clothes. Well, of course, it was a pile of clothes, but it was also a body.

Tyler looked back at Cal. "You're radiating enough alarm to make this a public broadcast."

"I know. I thought I could handle it." He rubbed his hand across his forehead, brushing back his unruly hair. "It just hit me when I stepped out there. And my screening broke down."

Tyler nodded slowly. "Take it easy," she said. She looked once again at the body crumpled at the other end of the hallway. "It isn't necessarily connected..." The discrepancy between her words and what she thought was too great for her to continue. She took a breath and began again. "Despite what we both feel, we really don't know that this is connected with the others." Cal didn't say anything, but it was clear he rejected Tyler's technicality. There was no doubt in his mind this was yet another in Jonas and the Chief's frightening series of deaths. Tyler said, "Stay here. I'll go find Jonas." They didn't need to acknowledge between them that Tyler's ability to screen was considerably more sophisticated than Cal's. Nor that many in the crowd gathered beyond the door were exceptionally perceptive.

The first thing Tyler caught visually when she re-entered the reception room was a glimmer of purple-green iridescence ascending the main stairs. Dorian's entourage had evidently dispersed. Only the cine actor, Ivor, she recalled irrelevantly, remained in attendance, and he and Dorian were obviously on their way out.

Tyler looked around but didn't see Jonas. In a crowd like this she couldn't attempt to find him psyonically, so she headed up the back stairway to get a view of the room. She finally spotted him in the corner diagonally opposite her. As she started to make the circuit of the room along the mezzanine, she saw him break off his conversation and continue toward the front stairway.

As if by pre-arrangement, the three of them seemed to be converging. Dorian, who had lingered at the top of the stairs. Jonas, who was approaching from the right. And Tyler, who was walking purposefully up the long end of the mezzanine. But Tyler stopped just short of the head of the stairs, positioning herself where Jonas could see her. He looked at her quizzically and she nodded. He hesitated a moment, glanced at Dorian, but then walked on to where Tyler waited. But Dorian, too, had seen Jonas. She turned to look after him and saw Tyler.

Dorian and Tyler stared at each other. They were too far apart and there was too much noise at all levels of perception for them to sort anything from each other. But Tyler watched as Dorian leaned forward to say something to the actor. He continued toward the main door but Dorian didn't accompany him.

When Jonas reached Tyler, he said, "I was trying to catch Dorian for a word before she left." Then he noticed the tightness in Tyler's face.

"I rather expect you'll have that," she said hoarsely. "Cal is waiting for you in the service corridor below us. They found a body."

Jonas looked confused, and then he looked shocked. "Here." His voice was thin and high.

"It's one of the maintenance workers. I don't know any details. Cal was on his way out to find you. He wasn't screening well, so I came instead."

Jonas seemed stunned, trying to absorb what he had been told. His reactions were almost automatic. "OK. You'd better wait up here somewhere." He looked around. "There are a couple of small lounges, just off the lobby." Jonas walked away quickly.

For Tyler, the confusion of the room seemed to rise to intolerable proportions.

Abruptly she closed out all psy perception and then turned away to find one of the small unoccupied lounges Jonas had mentioned. She went in and shut the door behind her. The sudden silence and solitude were like a balm.

The lounge was quietly lit. In its center, comfortable chairs were arranged around a low table. Tyler sat down and tried to convince herself that the dead maintenance worker wasn't necessarily going to be another one of Jonas' mystery deaths. But a sense of utter certainty kept intervening. Of course, he would be. He would fit the profile and make real the knowledge that in the course of the evening a murder had been committed, almost certainly by psyonic means.

It was sitting thus, absorbed in her own thoughts, that Dorian found her. "To use the kind of homely metaphor you might appreciate, you're closed as tight as a spring trap." Tyler realized Dorian must have been standing there a little time before she had spoken. Without breaking her careful screening, Tyler re-established psy perception. She was surprised to find what seemed to be genuine concern mixed with Dorian's usual amused detachment. Dorian gazed at Tyler assessingly. "Something's wrong. One might even speak melodramatically and say, disastrously wrong." When Tyler didn't answer, Dorian continued, "Might one know what it is?"

Tyler's face was very set and still. "Yes, I suppose one might." She echoed Dorian's mocking tone and inflection. Then in her own voice, she said, "I just learned someone's been found dead in one of the service corridors." And even as she spoke, she knew she was primarily waiting for Dorian's reaction.

There was no sudden burst of surprise or shock from Dorian. But then of course it was obvious she had been expecting something unpleasant. She shrugged. "That's unfortunate," she said without much expression, either inward or outward. "Who is it? What happened?"

Tyler shook her head, careful herself to reveal little. "I don't know. One of the maintenance people evidently. I came up to tell Jonas and he said to wait here."

Dorian studied Tyler. "You're very good. I suppose that's why Jonas picked you." Tyler's chin came up as if she were about to dispute, but Dorian didn't wait for denials. "Picked you for whatever it is that brought you here tonight. Picked you for whatever it is that has you...and Jonas...so upset. And now, really shaken." Dorian came over and sat in a chair directly opposite Tyler. The broad low table was between them. Dorian leaned back into the comfort of the chair, somehow managing to look both formal and relaxed at the same time. "Because you see, Tyler, I don't believe any of this pretense of ignorance. People dropping dead in back corridors, I grant you that makes a pretty unpleasant end to a festive evening. But such things happen. And while you'd be concerned, you wouldn't be...well, you wouldn't be like you are. Not unless it means a lot more to you than you want me to know." Dorian paused, but all she got from Tyler was a level stare and a continuation of her careful screening. "Should I leave, or will Jonas appreciate finding me here?"

At last Tyler smiled thinly. "I think we should both wait," she said.

"I had a hunch you'd say that."

So they waited, each withdrawn behind a screen of psy neutrality. But it was a neutrality, for Tyler at least, without rest or calm.

After a creeping passage of time which turned out to be twenty minutes or so, there came a muted babble of voices from the lobby. Tyler went to the door. She saw Doug Selnik in line at the front entrance, waiting to leave. Someone from building security was checking the names of everyone on their way out. Tyler wondered what excuse was being given for that. From Doug's disgruntled expression, it better be a good one. Further back Jonas, his face stiff, was ushering his wife toward the line, urgent whispers passing between them. And just outside the door to the lounge, making no effort to leave, stood Cal and Laurence. Even though they did not touch, Cal conveyed a proprietary attitude which gave the impression that Laurence was under guard.

For Tyler, the mental activity in the lobby came as a blur. Dominantly there was the reek of nervousness, the doubt of uncertainty, even the fascination of curiosity. Tired and anxiety ridden herself, she strained to sort specific responses but with little success. Then unexpectedly, rising out of the muddle like a rock tossed in a rushing river, came a fleeting sense of what might have been satisfaction or maybe even something stronger. Triumph? But even as she grasped for it, it was gone, swept away in the tumbling water. To vanish that quickly, it must have come from a psy, from someone who had screened that reaction immediately. Even as she tried to call back exactly what she had sorted, Tyler suddenly felt a strong uprush of that buzz of uneasiness she had been carrying with her ever since she had come into metro. Stay focused, try to pay attention, she reminded herself. But the rock, if it had ever been there, had disappeared, drowned in the innumerable bits of perception flooding around her. Frustrated, she was tempted to return to closure but she didn't. She felt she owed it to Jonas to remain psyonically receptive, no matter how futile her efforts seemed.

After seeing his wife off, Jonas came back toward the lounge. As he approached, he started to say something but Tyler broke in, "You're looking for Dorian. She's here."

He was surprised, but he didn't react outwardly. Instead he gestured to Cal and Laurence, ushering them into the lounge. Jonas closed the door. Dorian, who was the only one still seated, looked up at Jonas and said, "This reminds me of the scene where the brilliant investigator, having assembled his suspects, delivers the exposition which reveals the murderer." Alert and inquiring, Jonas turned to Tyler. But she just shrugged and shook her head.

Laurence moved his lips in disapproval. "That's in very poor taste, Dorian. As you know, some poor maintenance worker's dropped dead downstairs."

"What I don't know," Dorian said smoothly, "is why it's caused such a fuss."

Laurence's expression of disapproval deepened. But then he looked at Tyler and Jonas, and his expression changed. "Jonas?" he said.

"I'm sorry. I've got...things...to see to. Cal will tell you." Jonas backed out of the room, his haste obvious.

They all looked after him. Then Dorian turned her head toward the others. "The Commissioner seems anxious not to be in our company."

"And I must admit," Laurence joined in, looking at Tyler and Cal, "the two of you are reacting pretty strongly to all this."

Tyler ignored both comments. She said to Cal, "You've got a name."

"Yeah. Willis Crayton. Seems to have had a heart attack, stroke, something like that."

At the name, Tyler sorted a quick reaction of recognition from Laurence, but he screened it immediately. She couldn't tell whether either of the others had sorted his reaction as well. She almost wished she hadn't.

Cal particularly seemed to have directed his concentration totally to what he had to say and nothing more. "Jonas has asked me," he went on, "to ask you, all of you," he pointedly included Tyler, "to cooperate with the authorities in every way if...if they decide this is a matter which bears investigation." Sounding reluctant, he added, "The police have been notified."

"I don't need Jonas to remind me to act like a responsible citizen," Laurence said. It sounded pompous. He knew it and he made no apology for it. "But I do mean a responsible citizen. Not one who abrogates his rights for bureaucratic convenience."

Speaking to the air, Dorian said, "Thank you, Rights of Man."

Impatience shot through Laurence. "Your flippancy..." he started to say.

But Dorian looked at Cal and abruptly asked, "Did you find him?"

Inwardly, Cal responded with confusion, but he covered it quickly. "No. I..." It was obvious to the other three he was being careful to screen anything that lay behind his words. "I was standing near one of the service doors when one of the building security staff came out. I knew at once something was wrong. He showed me...we went to where Crayton was lying. One of the others on the maintenance crew had found him." Cal glanced at Tyler, his nervousness impossible to conceal. Dorian reacted with frank curiosity. Laurence's mood was more difficult to gauge, but it was obvious he too doubted the completeness of what they were being told. Cal continued. "Anyway I was on my way to find Jonas when..." His voice trailed off. He had caught his slip as soon as he made it.

Tyler caught it too but wasn't sure if the others had. She filled in. "I met Cal on his way. I was close to the service corridor door. Where we were sitting, Dorian. Anyway, I came instead of Cal."

Dorian's eyes gleamed with interest. She turned her attention to Cal. She hadn't missed his slip. "Why Jonas?" she asked. Cal looked anxiously at Tyler. "Why head straight for Jonas with the news?" Dorian asked again. "Instead of building security."

"I thought he should know. Immediately." Cal stammered a bit getting the words out.

Once again, Tyler cut in. "After all, Jonas does handle difficult situations as well as anyone."

"Is that what this is, a difficult situation?" This time it was Laurence who spoke and he allowed his skepticism to be fully evident.

"I suppose so," Tyler said, answering his challenge. "At least until they know for sure how the man died."

"Yes. I suppose that does need to be established."

"So in fact, I was right," Dorian said. "You and Jonas think this janitor could have been murdered. And for some reason we're the suspects." She seemed more fascinated than appalled.

Tyler shrugged. "Homicide is certainly a possibility the police need to eliminate. But in case they don't eliminate it, it's going to be a little late if they wait to check on the people who were here tonight."

Cal sighed. "Look, I think you're all running away with this a bit." Tyler noted that he managed to say it with conviction. "All we know is that one of the maintenance workers is dead. Apparently of natural causes. But that's got to be verified. And until it is, Enforcement wants to know who was here and to ask some questions. And Jonas would like us to cooperate. Fully."

"They going to question everybody?" Dorian asked.

"Eventually, I suppose," Cal said shortly.

"You suppose," Dorian echoed. "And do you also suppose there's any particular reason the only people still here, under your watchful eye, are the three CF4s who graced this gathering? And considering that one of them," she indicated Tyler, "was here as a command performance, that only leaves two...shall I say again, suspects."

There was a triumphant note within her that none of the others missed. But for Laurence, her speech had changed the focus of his attention. He stood, looking back and forth between Tyler and Cal.

"She's right, isn't she?" Then he spoke directly to Tyler. "You think this death is connected with what brought you to metro originally." At his words, Dorian's interest brightened like a flame. In Laurence, there was a moment of stillness, then he burst out, "One of you," his anger took in both Tyler and Cal, "I don't care which, tell us what's going on."

Tyler looked at him steadily. "There's nothing we can tell you," she said, letting the slightest emphasis float over the word *can*.

Before Laurence could reply, there was a sound of commotion in the hall. A man, not in uniform, but unmistakably an enforcement officer, stuck his head in the door. "I understand we have some people here willing to make statements," he said, his voice carefully neutral.

"Volunteers all," Dorian said. She stood up and they all moved toward the door. As they did, Dorian tapped Tyler on the arm. Give, Tyler, what's it about, she thought out carefully and precisely. Laurence sorted the unspoken words as well. Tyler just shook her head. The only emotions getting past her careful screening were weariness and a lingering gloom.

Chapter Thirteen

Laurence and Dorian left the now almost empty lobby with the plainclothes officer. They both noted only Cal accompanied them. Tyler stayed behind. When they had driven away, Jonas materialized. Without saying anything, he nodded in the direction of his ceevee. Tyler followed him.

Jonas and Tyler remained silent on the short trip across town, and continued so for a few minutes after they had settled into Jonas' office. They both seemed so overcome with weariness that for a time the only movement in the room were the curls of steam rising from the cups of coffee that sat, untasted, before them. To Jonas, Tyler appeared totally withdrawn. He suspected, but he wasn't sure, that she was in closure, blocking all psy perception. The silence stretched between them. Finally Jonas said quietly, "You OK?"

At first he doubted Tyler had heard him. She continued to gaze past him, staring intently at nothing. He started to repeat himself when he noticed her gaze had refocused on him. "It's all right, Jonas. I was just trying to get things straight." She reached for her coffee and sipped a little. Her movements were slow, almost languid.

"You're sure you're all right?"

"Oh, I'm fine," Tyler said with noticeable irony. "Considering we probably had another murder with questionable method tonight." She drank some more coffee. "And if so, one with Laurence and Dorian still in the thick of it." She sounded very tired.

"Maybe we could let this wait a bit," Jonas said doubtfully.

"Nice thought." Tyler closed her eyes briefly. When she opened them again, she said, "But more of a luxury than we can afford, I think."

"Yeah, I guess," Jonas replied. He reached for his apps pad. "Better record this." His voice sounded tentative. "Just for me and the Chief. Unofficially, of course."

Tyler took a sip of coffee. Then, with the cup cradled in her hands, she peered into it. Jonas was searching for a way to prompt her to begin when she looked up and said, "I had intended to report this evening in sequence, but you know the old line about best laid plans." She sensed in Jonas a considerable effort to patiently subdue his anticipation. "However," she smiled to herself, "the one hard fact I did learn keeps distracting me."

Jonas' effort to remain patient collapsed. "Tyler, this isn't one of your books. If you know something, tell me. Spare me the suspense."

"Calm down, Jonas. It's not much." She drank a little more coffee, then set the cup down. "All right, to begin at the end. Crayton's name. Laurence recognized it when he heard it. It startled him."

"Recognized it?" Jonas groped for the right conclusion. "Laurence knew Crayton?"

"No. I didn't say that. I don't know whether he knew Crayton or not. I can only say he knew the name."

Jonas gave a little sputter of exasperation. "Tyler, the name Willis Crayton is hardly a household word. It isn't likely Laurence would know the name without knowing the man." He smiled with a trace of condescension.

Tyler's expression hardened. "All I'm telling you, Jonas, is what I actually know from Laurence's response. Not what you might infer from it. I *know*," she put distinct emphasis on the word, "Laurence recognized the name. If you want to assume his recognition of the name means he knew the man, that's up to you. Just be clear, that's assumption, not knowledge."

Jonas caught the brusqueness in Tyler's tone. "Sorry, I didn't mean to be flip," he said. He thought about what she had said, then nodded. "OK, I guess I follow that distinction. But if Laurence recognized Crayton's name, that more or less lets him off the hook, doesn't it? If Laurence was surprised to find out it was Crayton who was dead, he couldn't have been the murderer."

Tyler shook her head. "It's the same thing I've just been telling you, Jonas. Laurence reacted to the name." Tyler stopped, trying to formulate an explanation. "It doesn't necessarily mean he knew the name belonged to the man lying dead in the hallway before he was told. All it means is he recognized the name. Not that the man and the name went together."

Jonas took a minute to work it out. "OK, OK, I think I follow you. You could kill someone whose name you didn't know. Then later when you found out the victim's name, discover that it was familiar."

"Yes," Tyler said emphatically.

"I don't know," Jonas said, his frustration clear, "it sounds a bit strained to me. You didn't get anything on where Laurence knew the name from, I suppose?"

Tyler shook her head again. "I warned you, you probably wouldn't be satisfied with the results of my inquiries tonight," she said.

"Did Laurence notice? That you sorted that recognition from him."

Tyler shrugged. "I'm not sure. But if he didn't, he'll probably remember later that he didn't screen immediately and he'll suspect I picked it up. I don't think Cal caught it though. I don't know about Dorian."

"Having Laurence and Dorian in the same building with one of the murders. It seems almost too convenient." Jonas bit at his thumb nail. "You think someone could be setting them up?"

Tyler ran her fingers across her forehead. "I don't know, Jonas. None of this makes much sense to me. The murders. If that's what they are. The motive. If there is any. Crayton's death. For which the place and time strike me as overly melodramatic."

"Still it seems we should have anticipated something like this," Jonas said with frustration.

"I don't see how," Tyler rejoined.

"I don't know...it just seems. After the fact, it seems so inevitable."

"That's the marvelous thing about hindsight." Tyler grimaced. "A word of singularly unpleasant imagery. Besides," she said, returning to the point, "we don't actually know yet that Crayton is another."

"Tell me something, Tyler. You really have any doubts left about Crayton, and the others?"

"No," she said with simple finality.

"Me either." Jonas fell silent, immersed in a mood somewhere between resignation and anger. Then he collected himself. "OK, so Laurence recognized Crayton's name. That's not much, but it's something. Anything else?"

"I'll try for my original plan. See if I can take this in order," Tyler began. "I talked to Laurence first. In fact he came looking for me. Which after his phone call last night didn't surprise me. He was quick to tell me he knew you were upset about something. That he'd assumed you'd called me in to help. He wanted to know what it was."

"Did you tell him?"

"No. Not in speech or psyonically. I did tell him his warning about Toller had been a little late, that Toller had already been in to see you."

"He didn't elaborate I suppose. About Toller, I mean."

"No. But he's worried about him. Of course, like you, he always worries about Toller. But this was more specific. Laurence came in this evening knowing more than he admitted." She sorted the frustration that rippled through Jonas again. "You have to understand, Jonas, between Laurence and myself, people with our psy level, well, Laurence could screen completely from me, but I'd know he was doing it. He didn't do that. But on the other hand, I don't think I sorted anything from him he intended to keep hidden. Except for the reaction to Crayton's name. As far as I can tell, that's the only thing that...slipped, if you will."

Jonas considered that for a while. "OK. Laurence admitted knowing something was up. He even called you last night to acknowledge that. And he reacted to Crayton's name. But we don't know what, if any connection, he sees between the two."

Tyler locked her hands behind her neck and leaned her head back against their support, her chin and elbows pointing in the air. "They're neither one of them stupid, Jonas."

"Laurence and Dorian," Jonas intoned needlessly.

Tyler let her hands pull her head forward so that she was looking at Jonas again. "Whatever we learned this evening, you can safely assume they've both figured out that Willis Crayton's death is more than simply an unfortunate blot on the evening's entertainment." She brought her arms down.

"I wish I knew exactly what information Laurence had," Jonas said. "And where he got it. I know he's got his sources, but this business hasn't exactly been a topic of departmental scuttlebutt." Jonas gave off a little tremor of worry and resentment.

"I did ask him whether he would submit to a full examination by Psy Management. Unofficially. If it were in the interest of public safety."

Jonas gave a smothered laugh. "His reaction to that must have been interesting."

"Yes, his answer was, if the Commissioner wants anything, he'll have to call a Demand. Make it official."

"Surprise, surprise."

"And that was about it. Laurence left, to see if he could get anything out of you."

Jonas shifted uncomfortably. "Yeah, I spent a good part of the evening avoiding him."

"You worry too much about that, Jonas." Tyler stopped, as if listening to something. And Jonas knew she was sorting his state of mind. He shifted position again. "Of course," she went on, "any psy perceiver who was around you this evening would know you're bothered by something. You carry anxiety around like an undercurrent. But nobody's going to know exactly what it is unless you tell them. Or carefully think it out in words. Remember Jonas..."

"I know, I know," Jonas burst out. "You keep reminding me, you read books, not minds. And I still contend that's easy for you to say."

"It's true, nonetheless. People don't usually go around thinking in carefully constructed sentences. Not unless they consciously decide to. What we mostly get is the effect things have on people, not the thing itself."

"I know that, I really do." This time Jonas spoke with quiet conviction, although his tone of voice still didn't quite match what he was feeling. "It's just awfully hard sometimes to keep what you feel from overpowering what you know."

"It's exactly in the difference between those two, Jonas, that psy perception normally functions. It's relatively easy to perceive what people feel. It's a little trickier to figure out exactly what they know." Tyler looked at him with some sympathy. "Although I do have to grant, you can infer quite a bit about causes when you have access to effects."

"So much for cheering me up," Jonas said sarcastically, but without any real edge to his voice. He drained his coffee cup and rubbed his eyes wearily. "So, what about Dorian?" he asked.

"Like Laurence, she assumed I was at the reception for a reason. Part of the reason being to buttonhole her. And like Laurence, she made it easy. She sought me out for conversation. By the end of which, she made it a point to tell me she knew you were extremely bothered by something. And that the 'something' had to do with impartment." Jonas became instantly alert. "But with Dorian," Tyler added quickly, "all that, I think, was a matter between her and me." Jonas looked at Tyler quizzically. Tyler took a breath as if to continue speaking, but no words came out. After a pause, she finally said, "It seems unlikely, moving as we do in completely different orbits, but there's always a sense of competition between us. And that's how she seemed to take this, as if my presence had created a puzzle for her to solve. At one point, she appeared to drop all screening. I'd be tempted to swear when we started talking she didn't know the substance of the matter and her only interest was to see how much she could find out for herself. But to return to my earlier distinction, that's inference, not knowledge."

"Could she fool you, Tyler? About what she knows."

"In a social setting like that, yes, I'm certain she could. So could Laurence for that matter."

"You think of anything else?"

Tyler stared vacantly past him for a while. Something about the evening was nagging at the back of her mind, but she couldn't quite bring it to awareness. Instead she said, as if offhandedly, "Interesting, and I suppose fortunate, that Cal was on the scene so promptly."

"Yes, at least we had some control over the situation." Tyler could feel the sudden click within Jonas. "Tyler. Cal?" He sat for a moment, flabbergasted. "You don't suspect Cal? That's impossible."

"I don't suppose I do. But I'd be curious to know where he was when the other bodies turned up."

"Cal has no record of impartment ability," Jonas said indignantly. Tyler knew he was offended, as if his judgment had been attacked, his judgment which considered Cal absolutely trustworthy.

"We've mentioned the possibility of an unregistered high level psy. Mis-registration is also possible," she said quietly.

Resistance rose in Jonas like a wall. "I won't believe it."

"Jonas, you cannot make your fear of the possibility a barrier to examining all the facts." Jonas' face remained as set and stony as his mood. Tyler pressed the point. "The registration and rating of psy capability may be a marvelous piece of technology. But it's no more infallible than any other technology."

"We consider the possibility of error in psy ratings as statistically irrelevant." Jonas was angry.

"Jonas." Tyler gave him a challenging stare, and his anger broke.

"I'm sorry, Tyler. Truly. You're doing what I asked you to do. You shouldn't have to put up with my temper when it makes me uncomfortable. Still the accuracy of psy ratings is, if not infallible, damn close to it."

"'Statistically insignificant,'" Tyler quoted. "That's the word they use, not 'irrelevant.' And it also refers to the distribution of psy capability in the population at large. So you'll pardon me if this other statistical insignificance, this point naught naught naught possibility of error looms somewhat large in my mind." Jonas could not feel the relentless tenacity in Tyler but he knew it was there. It was one of the characteristics which had led him to call on her in the first place. "So do you have a proximity report on Cal?" she asked.

"No." Jonas looked down, almost in a gesture of defeat. "But I'll get one."

Tyler relented a little. "Jonas. I don't think Cal is a murderer. Come to that, I don't think either Laurence or Dorian is either. But we've both got to face the fact that what we think in this matter is largely the result of what we feel. What we want to be true." She slumped back slightly in her chair. "We don't want any of this to be true. Maybe if we collect all the pieces, we'll get our wish and it'll all go away. But whatever, the only way out of this, is through it."

"God, Tyler. If we don't solve this." Jonas tried to still the tumult within him, but he could not. "I don't know. I just don't know." Tyler recoiled from the onslaught of fear and anxiety in him but she did not close off her perception of it. When Jonas had regained most of his composure, he said, "That's enough for tonight. Why don't you go back to your hotel, and I'll have somebody pick you up in the morning."

"And you, you going home?"

"No, I'll just catch a little sleep here."

As she got up to leave, Tyler asked, "Jonas, you haven't ever felt personally threatened in this case, have you?"

Jonas looked up, and Tyler sorted genuine surprise in him. "Me. No. Why would I?"

"No reason I suppose. Except that you're non-psy and you're playing a pretty pivotal role. It just seemed to me you could possibly become a target."

Jonas jumped to a quick conclusion. "You've been talking to Meryl, haven't you?"

"I'm supposed to be the telepath, Jonas, not you. Anyway your wife and I, we just exchanged a few words at the reception. She's worried about you."

"She can usually tell when something's really getting to me. What did you say to her?"

"I told her I didn't think you were in any danger. But since then, I've been trying to convince myself I was right."

Chapter Fourteen

Tyler left and was driven back to her hotel. The rest of that night she spent in restless, dream-ridden sleep. She dreamed someone was calling her name across a void of space. And that fact was very important. Not that she answered, which she did not. But that someone called to her.

Finally near dawn, she awoke to the consciousness of what her mind was seeking. A scene formed. She was standing in the door of the small lounge outside the reception hall, watching the swirl of activity and feeling the anxious tremors of the people who filed to the exit or lingered in the lobby. Out of the restless scene, a tableau emerged, one moment of stasis. Doug Selnik near the door. Jonas shepherding his wife. Cal keeping close to Laurence. Dorian's presence in the room behind her. And then as quickly the scene broke again into a clutter of motion, physical and pysonic. Doug had passed — through the security check. Jonas' wife had joined the line at the door. Jonas, Cal and Laurence had come into the lounge.

When the scene dispersed, Tyler was fully awake. She got up and crossed to the window. She opened the drapes on the first cool light of morning not yet touched by the sun.

She remembered, somewhere in that frozen moment she thought she had sorted, for an instant, that someone was very pleased with themselves. But that perception had vanished as quickly as it had come. It had been blotted out, quickly screened, then replaced by an inner voice, a voice urgent and commanding, telling her to pay attention. Focus. Pay attention to what you always hear. And her awareness had slid seamlessly back to that general background noise of disquiet, her constant companion since her arrival in metro. At the time, she had assumed it was only her own anxiety surfacing. But now she wasn't so sure. It seemed to her she might have sorted someone else's thought. As if someone else were insistently reminding themselves to concentrate, to keep focused. If so those urgent thoughts, whether her own or someone else's, had overridden anything else she might have been able to perceive.

Tyler groped to reconstruct the moment before her own perception had shifted, to recall more clearly that flash of something which had slipped past someone's screening. But whose? Who had acted so quickly to screen something they had not wanted anyone to sort?

Most likely it was one of the four people closest to her. Dorian, Laurence, Cal, Jonas. Tyler's reconstruction stopped abruptly. Of course, only three, three psy perceivers, not four. Only Dorian, Laurence, and Cal. Still her mind stubbornly insisted on linking Jonas with them. But certainly that was to be expected. Jonas was inseparable from this matter, at least as far as she was concerned.

Beyond that...no...she could no more suspect Jonas than she could suspect herself. And that he could be an unregistered psy, that was quite simply impossible. Tyler stopped herself. How would that measure up against all her preaching about the difference between knowledge and inference? Not very well perhaps, but still she would not believe it. Could not believe it, that Jonas could be an unregistered psy perceiver. And not discovered through all these years. Still there was nothing particular in the way people thought and felt that marked psy from non-psy. You knew you were dealing with other psy when they revealed to you what they were perceiving and sometimes by their evident screening of the things they didn't want you to know about. But a high level psy who was careful could deliberately conceal both those activities. And in the case of someone not identified as psy, you wouldn't know they were screening because you wouldn't be looking for it in the first place.

Damn, she thought. This is crazy. Pushing aside what had to be a futile line of speculation, Tyler again tried to recapture that moment just before someone's screening had clicked into place, but her thoughts spiraled like the funnel of water in a whirlpool. She felt much like a panicked swimmer who was being pulled down to the bottom.

She had been standing at the window a long time, long enough for the morning light to have warmed. Somewhere the sharper recollection she was groping for probably held. Maybe in time it would surface, but it would not be forced. Mentally she gave herself the image of a dog shaking off water. She turned from the window, ordered breakfast, dressed and waited for the ceevee from Psy Management to arrive.

It took her directly to Enforcement. She was shown immediately into Chief Wilkins' office. Jonas was with him. On the Chief's large flat panel was the image of a Statistics and Probability graph. The atmosphere was tense and Tyler's arrival only caused it to tighten a little more.

Once Tyler was seated, Wilkins picked up in the middle of what he had been saying. "I've just been telling Jonas, we've confirmed that Crayton's death fits our pattern." He gestured to the graph. The probability line which ascended in bright red came up to but did not cross the discreet gray line that ran horizontally. "So that brings us right up to the turn for the probability of homicide."

"What about method?' Jonas asked. Tyler felt the jump of anxiety within him. "Anything new on method?" His voice sounded flat.

Wilkins touched his apps pad and the display changed to include the now all-too-familiar list of names. Above the list, flamboyantly blinking on and off were the words "Data Conflict." Below it: "All probable homicides. Next input will reach statistical certainty zone. No method determined. Hypothetical projection for pysonic — impartment as method conforms with all data. No other conforming projections."

Wilkins' brown eyes were deep and assessing. "I don't guess I have to translate."

Tyler's head moved slightly, more a twitch than a gesture of negation. "What are you going to do about Laurence and Dorian?" she asked.

"That's part of what we've got to decide right now," Wilkins said. "Especially since this is a sample of what I've got to contend with." With a quick stab, he touched the play icon. Dorian's voice, set to just the right combination of arrogance, self-assurance, and sarcasm, filled the room.

"As a conscientious citizen, naturally I accept it as my responsibility to cooperate with public officials in the performance of their duties. But I fail to see what else you expect of me. I have given a full account of my actions this evening. If the death of this janitor appears suspicious to you, doubtless you have your reasons for viewing it in that light. But I assure you, there is nothing I can tell you that will assist you. I should think an interview with your medical examiners would be far more productive."

On the recording, Chief Wilkins spoke. "Preliminary examination suggests some form of stroke." His voice was gravelly and just short of angry.

"As I said, I'm sure you have your reasons for," Dorian's voice paused as if she had been searching for just the right expression, "extending your investigations beyond the limits of the preliminary report. But now, unless you have anything further, I really must bring this interview to a close." There was a momentary gap before Dorian's voice resumed. "I think you should know that on Wednesday next, I begin a project for IsogaCorp. It'll probably keep me occupied for some time. I won't fly back just to repeat what I've already told you. So if you do need anything further from me, contact me before I leave on Tuesday."

Chief Wilkins touched the stop icon. "D. Rath is sending some clear messages. And I don't need psy perception to pick them up. One message is that officially, right now, we have no hold on her. The other is that by the middle of the week she's going to be in multinational corporate domain. If we file any official warrants then, we'll have to go through federal diplomacy to extradite if she decides not to return willingly to Philly Sector jurisdiction."

"What about Laurence?" Jonas asked.

"About the same. In slightly different words. He'll cooperate, within the limits of the law. But not beyond." Wilkins looked at Tyler. "Your...ah...colleagues...don't seem very public spirited."

"Can you blame them? Given the circumstances," Tyler replied. "After all if they are innocent, presumably they don't have enough knowledge to fully grasp what we're dealing with."

"You think that's still true, after Crayton's death?" Wilkins asked.

"You've already listened to our conversation, Jonas' and mine, from last night." Chief Wilkins nodded. "As I said, Dorian and Laurence," Tyler went on, "they can figure out a lot. But that's not the same as knowing what the three of us know." As she spoke, she looked at the display showing the probability graph and the list of names.

"And I still think," Jonas said, "if Laurence won't cooperate, we should give him what we've got. Then he won't have much excuse for standing on formalities. And I don't see that we've got anything to lose. Whoever's guilty already knows all of this anyway."

"It's more complicated than that, Jonas," Wilkins said. "Right now, besides ourselves, only the murderer knows about all the deaths. And identifying that someone has that level of knowledge can be vital to an investigation. Sharing it with my chief suspects denies me an important hook." Wilkins turned his attention back to Tyler. "But you are sure about Meredith recognizing Crayton's name?" He sounded doubtful

"Yes. I'm sure."

After a pause and still looking at Tyler, Chief Wilkins said, "Don't know if it's necessary to mention it, but we've sent for him. Meredith, I mean."

Tyler smiled. "Actually I did pick that up, but if I hadn't, I would have assumed you'd want to talk to him again." She shifted her gaze between Jonas and the Chief. "There is something else, something that's not on the recording. I couldn't quite place it last night. And it's probably nothing. But at the end of the evening there in the lobby, I'm pretty sure I sorted something," Tyler hesitated, "something I lost too quickly. Something somebody made sure they screened very promptly. "

"What was it?" the Chief asked.

Tyler shrugged. "It lasted only a couple of seconds but it seemed like someone felt very pleased with themselves. As if they had accomplished something." She felt Jonas' surprise, but from the Chief there was only sharp intentness. After a pause she added, "Of course, that's hardly an unusual reaction after an event that's as much professional as social."

Watching her, Chief Wilkins said, "But..."

"I don't know. It seemed especially urgent somehow, the way someone blocked that reaction. The next thing, all I sorted was someone telling themselves to concentrate. Which only reminded me that was what I needed to do. It felt like someone covered their slip very conveniently. In a way that made me turn my own thoughts inward." She stopped there. She didn't mention her recollection that she had also felt an uprise in that background hum she carried around with her. She still felt an aversion to discussing, even with Jonas much less with the Chief, that sense of subtle yet persistent disquiet which dogged her.

Quietly Wilkins asked, "If you're right about somebody trying to hide something from you, could it have been Laurence Meredith or Dorian Rath?"

"It could have been. They were close to me." She shot a glance at Jonas. "Cal Houlston was too." Jonas clicked his teeth in disgruntlement. Tyler went on. "But it could have been almost any psy milling around near the door. Anyway I'm probably making too much of it. Countering a lapse in screening, anybody would do that. Doesn't mean there was anything sinister about it."

Wilkins said, "Still if this was a deliberate attempt to distract you, that's something we've got to consider."

"Still wouldn't make whoever did it a murderer," Tyler said.

"Tyler." Jonas said on a wave of skepticism. "You just don't want it to be true." Chief Wilkins felt the same but with a hint of reservation. Tyler wondered if it were sympathy on his part or just the policeman's professional awareness of the difference between probability and certainty.

Tyler let out a long breath. "I said last night, none of this makes much sense. And the more I think about it, the less sense it makes." Her own frustration and irritation had surfaced. She turned abruptly to Jonas. "Tell me, Jonas, what happens if we don't clear this up and it becomes publicized?" There was a burst of exasperation from Jonas, but Tyler didn't wait for it to form into words. She went on, "A veritable firestorm of anti-psy feeling. Right? And probably not just violence of feeling either. Why in the hell would any psy perceiver want that?" Tyler's voice was harsh. "That's what doesn't make any sense to me. You've posited a method which only a psy could use. At the same time, it's creating a result which no psy would want."

"No psy who's sane, at any rate," Jonas said. "But I don't think we're dealing with sanity, Tyler."

"All right, but if we're not, that means either Laurence or Dorian is crazy. And has managed to beat the profiles. Or it means there's a mis-registered, or unregistered, psy perceiver who's done the same thing. Who also happens to be crazy. Why don't you run some probabilities on the likelihood of any of that being true."

"Tell me, Tyler," Chief Wilkins interjected, "can you think of any rational motive for a psy who had the ability to murder people by the power of the mind, can you think of a rational motive for doing it? For running the risk of creating a devastating anti-psy panic?" It suddenly occurred to Tyler that the Chief had been waiting to ask that question for a while. It was also evident to her he had already formulated an answer.

She echoed his thought. "You'd run that risk if you thought the alternative was worse."

Jonas almost shouted, "That's ridiculous." He lowered his voice but not his level of emotion. "Anyway you're both talking as if there could be a rational basis for these murders. There isn't. They're random, with no more motive than someone's deluded brain."

"Maybe so," Wilkins said, "but I ran some of those other probabilities Tyler asked about. And they say the possibility that a high level psy perceiver could be an impulse driven maniac and conceal that mental imbalance from the profiles, that prob stands at just about nil."

"An unregistered psy wouldn't have a profile," Jonas said stubbornly.

The Chief looked at him steadily. "As for that probability, the one that hypothesizes the existence of a PsyCF4 who's both unregistered *and* a homicidal maniac, that one's even closer to zero. All of which leaves us..." A rap on the door interrupted him. "That's probably Meredith," he said.

But the officer who entered was alone. "We weren't able to locate L. Meredith. He didn't turn up at his apartment last night. The people in his office at the League *say*," the officer put a firm inflection on the word, "they haven't heard from him."

"You think they're lying?" the Chief asked.

"I think he's been in touch with someone there today," the officer answered.

Jonas reacted quickly. "I'll send Cal over. See what he can find out."

"No." the Chief said. "Sorry, Jonas, but I'm not going to wait on this. I'm processing an interrogation warrant for Laurence. Now."

Chapter Fifteen

After the last half hour with Jonas and Chief Wilkins, Tyler should have welcomed a return to the solitude of her hotel suite. Unfortunately she didn't. Their final discussion had been clamorous, both in words and in feelings. Jonas had argued long and hard against taking any official steps with regard to Laurence, but the Chief had remained unmoved. He had, however, assured Jonas that he would treat the interrogatory on Laurence as cautiously as possible. Despite that assurance, Jonas had left Enforcement, unconvinced and unsatisfied. Almost as unsatisfied as Tyler herself who felt her involvement had been distressingly futile. At least from Jonas' point of view. If the purpose of calling her in had been to gather information discreetly, the one piece of information she had provided, Laurence's recognition of Crayton's name, had led to an opposite result.

It had all left her irritated with them and with herself. She decided, rather than going straight back to the hotel, she might ease her mood by getting out at the far side of the park and walking the rest of the way. The park had become her habit since she had been in metro. It eased her homesickness for her own environment and was worth that small trembling of generalized psy perception which stayed with her and quieted only when she was alone in her rooms.

As she had done before, she stopped and sat for a while in the circle of the Riscoll Monument. Inwardly Tyler laughed at herself. This spot had become her security blanket, it seemed. Silly to need one, sillier still to have chosen this place. But she had to admit that the park, this meager concession to grass and trees by the world of brick and concrete, did seem to offer some solace. A place to sift through thoughts. And somehow it seemed ironically appropriate to do that, in this case, in the shadow of the memory of D. Hollins Riscoll.

She reviewed all she had shared with Jonas and Chief Wilkins. Particularly she tried to reconstruct the moment of Laurence's reaction to Crayton's name, to search it for Laurence's exact response. His recognition had been unquestionable despite his quick screening. But the attendant emotion, had he been shocked, surprised? Startled was probably the most accurate word, but as she had told Jonas and the Chief, startled at the name, not necessarily at the fact of the death.

And then there surfaced in Tyler an impression she had avoided, maybe repressed. Laurence hadn't just been startled by Crayton's name. Hearing it had also brought to him a fleeting sense of satisfaction, as if he were pleased that the name Willis Crayton matched with someone who was dead. She thought for a while, trying to decide how sure she was about that reaction. Not sure enough to call Jonas, or the Chief. Not immediately anyway. Besides it wouldn't change the urgency with which they sought for Laurence. The Chief already wanted him badly enough. Thanks to her.

She examined that response in herself and found guilt as certainly as she had found recognition in Laurence. Rationally she knew cooperating with Jonas was right. Ethical. Moral. Whatever. But her intuition protested. And it seemed her protest arose from something more than a sense of betraying her friendship with Laurence. It went deeper than that, to a sense of being pulled between opposing sides. She resented that feeling because she believed there should be no such opposition. No conflict between civic responsibility and loyalty, not just to Laurence, but to other psy perceivers as well. Only she had to admit to herself that there was.

Tyler smiled ruefully at the stolid hunk of stone before her. You did reasonably well, D. Hollins Riscoll, she thought, but you didn't solve all the problems. Nor could you.

Her perception of another's constant broke into her meditations. With a crunch of footsteps on the gravel path, a man walked by. They exchanged glances and polite public smiles. He was well-dressed, good-looking, a corporate or professional. As he passed, he focused for a moment on the monument. A burst of emotion flared in him, hot, raw, not careless like the reaction of the man with the family group the other day. His response carried such intensity that Tyler actually flinched. It was hatred, resentment, and deep anger, all called forth by the reminder of psy perception which the monument had given him. Tyler had experienced that reaction before, not frequently, but often enough. And though in this case it was directed not at her personally, but at psy perceivers in general, it left her even more saddened and disturbed.

More discouraged than she had been, Tyler got up and started back to the hotel. She had reached the gateway across from the front entrance when her phone sounded. She checked it. It was a text from Cal. "Toller news conference. Call you after."

"Damn it," Tyler said, louder than she intended.

She checked her apps pad. A solemn faced announcer was giving the usual set up. "We interrupt our regularly scheduled programming for breaking news." Tyler knew she wanted to watch Toller on a full screen, so she quickened her pace. She didn't quite run which might have gotten an "anything wrong?" query from the guard in the security kiosk but she walked rapidly.

When she got to her room, she selected vid, and the wall panel filled with Hardin Toller's face, carefully composed into lines of public gravity. He was just beginning his opening statement. "I call upon Chief Wilkins to remember his primary duty is to the majority of citizens in this metro, to their protection and well-being. The death of Willis Crayton may have occurred naturally." The skepticism of Toller's tone denied the words. "But I have information, confidential information, to suggest that Willis Crayton may have been murdered. While he labored in back hallways, while the influential and the powerful pursued their own interests, he died. Perhaps at the hands of an assassin.

"I call upon Chief Wilkins to bring the full brunt of his investigative apparatus to bear upon the death of this poor unfortunate. Willis Crayton had no power, no influence. Willis Crayton had no one to defend him, no one to speak for him.

"But I speak for him and for all like him. For we are all Willis Crayton, all of us who are ordinary and normal citizens." His inflection was masterful. "And I call upon Chief Wilkins particularly to inform us what Enforcement wants with PsyCF4 Laurence Meredith for whom an interrogatory warrant was issued within the last two hours. What connection is there, Chief Wilkins, between Laurence Meredith and the death of Willis Crayton? Laurence Meredith who heads the most powerful and influential pro-psy organization in this country. That is a question the citizens of this metro require that you answer.

"But there is another, even graver, question before us." Toller's voice grew more heavy and portentous. "Willis Crayton's death, tragic though it may be, is not our only concern. Because Willis Crayton's death may not be an isolated case. Are there others?" The camera drew in close upon Toller. His face had the look of a hunter who had put up with the frustration of pursuing an invisible quarry and suddenly found that quarry in sight. "Are there other deaths, those in authority, those who should protect us, know," he repeated the word and his inflection rose to hammer it, "know are undoubtedly connected? What other deaths, besides Willis Crayton's, should they be telling us about?" It seemed as if he would add something, but he simply stopped, his final question left hanging, its challenge unmistakable.

In the question and answer session that followed, the reporters pursued the source of Toller's confidential information. And Toller exploited that fully. "Of course, I cannot, at this time, reveal any more." With great solemnity he added, "You realize the life of my informant might be at stake."

An insistent voice among the reporters rose to the surface. "Legislator Toller, do you really believe this man Crayton was murdered? And if you do, can you tell us the names of the others with whom you believe his death is connected?"

With smooth satisfaction, Toller answered, "Those are questions for Chief Wilkins and Enforcement to answer." Then more harshly he threw back, "And here are some others. Does Wilkins have reason to believe a series of heretofore unacknowledged homicides has been committed? Does he have a reason for postponing the opening of an official investigation in the face of what may be a series of deaths of questionable circumstance?" Toller's voiced dropped to sleekness again. "Understand I, like you, can only ask these questions. It is Chief Wilkins who can answer them."

The reporters pressed Toller for additional names but all they got in return were flourishes about security and civic responsibility. Tyler assumed that meant Toller had not yet satisfied himself about whatever information he had. The real purpose of the news conference was probably to see what kind of reaction he could provoke from Wilkins.

The reporters' questions continued, most of them variations on things which had already been asked, all of them allowing full range for Toller's rhetoric.

Tyler had to grant, Toller knew how to play a house for all it was worth, but at last the performance concluded. An announcer's voice, fairly quivering with urgency, cut in, "Now we switch to Enforcement Headquarters where Chief Isa Wilkins is ready to issue a statement."

Chief Wilkins' smooth, brown face managed to convey a sense of tolerant boredom, a busy man patiently wasting his time on unimportant details. "As most of you know, last night during the opening reception for the annual conference held by the Association to Promote Cooperative Understanding, a maintenance worker named Willis Crayton was found dead. His body was discovered in a service corridor by other building personnel. Preliminary medical examination indicates stroke as the cause of death. However it is standard procedure in such cases to investigate fully, to eliminate any possibility that anything other than natural causes was involved. We are pursuing those investigations at this time and expect to have them completed within a day."

"Chief. Chief." They were different reporters than the ones who had questioned Toller, but their voices were the same. Chief Wilkins leaned almost out of the image frame to consult an aide. "All right. We do have time for a few questions, but just a few."

"Chief, what about Laurence Meredith? Why did you put out an interrogatory on him?"

Wilkins assumed a look of bland surprise. "We have additional questions to ask him, of course?"

"Any truth to Legislator Toller's allegations that Crayton's death might be connected to others?"

"No. Not that we know of." Wilkins lied with calm assurance. "Of course, if Legislator Toller has any information he thinks would be of use to us, we'd certainly be happy to have it."

"Why is Meredith the only person on whom you've put an official interrogatory?"

"As I said, we have some follow up inquiries we wish to make."

"So Meredith is the only one you wish to question further?"

"Yes. At this time. If other matters come up, we'll certainly issue other interrogatories, if necessary. At this point, we're simply following standard procedure."

"You're saying an interrogatory is standard procedure in a case like this?" The reporter made no attempt to disguise his skepticism.

Chief Wilkins replied in a tone of patient instruction. "When we can't immediately locate the person we wish to question, yes." He paused as if giving time for the explanation to sink in, but continued again just as other questions were being called out. "You have to understand, after our preliminary discussions last night, L. Meredith undoubtedly had no way of knowing we wanted to reach him today for further assistance in our investigation." The Chief's face broadened into a smile. "Of course, I'm sure he does now. Thanks to your able assistance." His glance took in the assemblage of reporters. A ripple of laughter arose. Before it subsided, the Chief said, much more brusquely. "All right. One more now." He singled out a reporter by name, a tall angular woman with a halo of frizzy hair. "Yes, you, J. Manetti."

"Isn't all this quite a fuss over someone who presumably dropped dead of natural causes?"

"Yes. I think you're probably right. But then again, I didn't create the fuss. As I said, Enforcement's been following standard procedure. Contrary to some people's opinions, we do investigate when ordinary citizens turn up dead in public places. Unfortunately it's not all that rare an occurrence. Usually nobody pays any attention. Except for us. In this case, Willis Crayton died during a well-publicized function. We understand that attracts a little more attention. To the best of our knowledge at this time, he died of natural causes. And after we tie up a couple of loose ends, I'm confident that's going to be the finding of our investigation."

With flawless timing, Chief Wilkins stepped back as his aide stepped forward. Wilkins was already on his way out, flanked by a couple of officers, as the aide announced, "Thank you, media representatives. That's all for now."

The beep of Tyler's phone interrupted the announcer's summary. She expected it to be Cal, but it was Dorian's face which now filled the display. "What in the hell was that all about?" she demanded, her voice as sharp as her acid green eyes.

"I assume you mean the media show we've just had."

"I mean Crayton's death and what Enforcement wants with Laurence. Because you do know, Tyler. It's got to do with Jonas, and why you turned up at the reception."

A gentle tone sounded in the background. Tyler said, "I've got another call."

"You're popular today. It's probably Jonas."

Tyler checked the incoming number. It was Cal but she didn't correct Dorian. "I need to take it. And anyway there's really nothing else I can tell you."

"Yeah. Well, it doesn't take any great brilliance to figure out they think Crayton was murdered. What's really scary is Toller hatching conspiracy theories. That might not bother me quite so much, except you and Jonas were already up to something, before Crayton was found. That's why you were there last night. Tell me, Tyler, did you and Jonas expect something to happen?" But Dorian ended the call without waiting for either an answer or an evasion.

Tyler touched call pending and the other call came through. Cal's image showed anxious eyes. Small worry lines creased the space between his eyebrows. "Who was that?"

"Dorian."

"Wanting...?"

"Wanting to know what's going on, of course?"

Cal was silent for a time. "You know, Tyler, sometimes I wonder whether we're handling this correctly at all."

"I'm not sure I see a lot of options."

"Maybe you're right. Anyway Jonas said, we should just sit tight for a while."

The third call, audio only, video blocked, came about an hour later. Somehow Tyler wasn't really surprised. "Laurence," she said when she heard his voice. "Where are you?"

"I'd rather not say."

"Your absence is conspicuous."

"More like suspicious, you mean. Interrogatories. Hardin Toller. The whole bit." A brief silence hung between them. "Anyway, I want to meet with you. Alone." Tyler hesitated. "You scared, Tyler, to meet with me?"

"No. That's not what's bothering me." Perhaps somewhat surprisingly, Tyler realized that was true. It wasn't Laurence, but the middle ground between two loyalties which seemed frightening. It also seemed inevitable. "All right, Laurence. Where?"

Before answering, Laurence asked, "Jonas isn't doing real time gps tracking on you, is he?"

"No," Tyler said curtly.

"How about direct surveillance?"

"No one's following me." Tyler's voice rose impatiently. "At least no one from Jonas. Or from Wilkins."

"If you're sure," Laurence said blandly, "why don't you go over to Now and Then Books. Browse around for a while." Without adding anything more, he ended the call.

Now and Then Books. Tyler had to admit to herself Laurence had chosen well. It was her favorite source for old print books. Although she regularly browsed its extensive inventory online, she usually made it a point to visit the store when she was in metro.

Tyler arrived at Now and Then about half an hour after she had talked to Laurence. As she strolled in, Terrence Grady intercepted her. He was the owner and manager. And he was PsyCF2. "If it isn't Tyler West." He drawled the words in exaggerated surprise. A surprise which Tyler immediately sorted existed only in his words. Laurence had set things up very well.

"TG," she acknowledged.

"I could almost consider this an honor, Tyler. Your appearances are becoming so rare."

"I have a few days of...business...in metro," she said dryly.

"So I heard," he returned with equal dryness. It was the kind of exchange familiar to psy perceivers. Grady realized Tyler would know he had been expecting her, that Laurence had forewarned him of her arrival. With his CF2 rating, there was no way he could screen well enough to prevent her from sorting that information and he made no attempt to. Still he spoke as if her arrival were unanticipated.

Grady led the way past the racks which filled the front of the store. They held readers and commcards containing editions with the special features which weren't licensed for a standard ebook download. Beyond the racks comfortable chairs and low tables were spread around. Gathered at one of the tables, four people with readers in hand were deep in earnest discussion. Along one of the sidewalls, doors led to the rooms equipped for 3D projection where Grady's customers could interact with life-sized versions of their favorite characters. On the opposite wall was a coffee bar. Grady always said, he actually made his money off lattes and cappuccinos. According to him, their profit margin was better even than the 3D enactments.

As Grady walked with Tyler toward the back room which housed the print books, he gestured to one of the many display panels hanging on the walls. With a series of morphing images, it was advertising Tyler's latest. Glancing at it, he said, "You'll be glad to know, your stuff always sells well."

"That's very gratifying."

"Not that you need the money, of course."

"I don't know what's worse for calling attention to yourself," Tyler said, "being psy or being rich."

"If the burden of the latter ever gets to be too much for you, I'd be glad to help you out. Take some of the boodle off your hands." Grady was greatly amused by his own joke.

"Thanks, TG, I'll try to remember that."

Opening the door to the back room, Grady pointed to a nearby bank of shelves. "Some new arrivals there," he said.

Tyler lost herself for a while wandering among the rows of printed books. She liked the sight of them, their spines in line, thick and thin, short and tall. Some colorful in dust jackets, others somber in covers only. She liked having her eyes caught by a word in a title, pulling the book out of its place, hefting it in her hands, turning the pages. Still despite her apparent absorption, when Laurence approached, she sensed him before she saw him.

"Ever get the urge to see one of yours done like that?" he asked as he came up to her.

She slid the book she had been looking at back into its place on the shelf. "Not really," she said, turning to face him. "Seems to me it'd be a little like a twentieth century writer wanting her book hand copied on parchment."

"You've always had a taste for old-fashioned things, Tyler."

"I like space and I like the natural world. The old-fashionedness is a means, not an end."

Laurence waited a few moments, sorting what he could from her. At last he nodded, somewhat absently. "Let's go." He headed for the back where there was an exit.

"Hold it a minute," Tyler said. She leaned around the doorway which led to the front. "TG," she called. "I'll take that first edition of *Gaudy Night*. Put it aside for me." Then she followed Laurence out the back.

Chapter Sixteen

Laurence had a ceevee waiting. He had evidently already programmed their destination. The car threaded its way through the streets, finally stopping at a plaza located outside Philly Sector's central core. In the afternoon before the end of the Saturday workday and the start of the weeksend, the plaza was not crowded with shoppers, but it wasn't exactly deserted either.

Laurence led the way to a bench in one of the small shaded courtyards set between the stores. As they sat down, Laurence said, "You'd probably prefer something more isolated, but I like nondescript public places for private meetings."

"You do this often? Playact like a character in a quikvid thriller?" Tyler's sarcasm was undisguised.

"Maybe I picked it up from the Commissioner. You know, your friend Jonas." There was anger in Laurence, but it seemed almost calculated, as if to hide something else. Anxiety, perhaps. "I don't much like the position I've been put in," he finished.

"More like the one you've put yourself in," Tyler said. "Why in the world have you gone into hiding?" She knew Laurence would sort her exasperation.

He did and it seemed to provoke a more genuine anger in him. A sudden pallor washed the warmth from his light brown skin. The much deeper brown of his eyes darkened. "Maybe I'm not as dutiful a citizen as you are. Or maybe I have something to hide," he said with deliberate challenge. Then he blew out a long breath. Recovering his calm, he said more quietly, "Or maybe because I'm not quite ready to share everything I know with Jonas. In his official capacity. Not until I know what's going on, anyway."

"And that's what you want from me. To know what's going on."

"Yes, in fact."

"Or at least to know more than you know already," Tyler said flatly.

Laurence rubbed the palm of one hand across the back of the other. Then he said, "We both know Jonas and Wilkins suspect me of something. On top of which, I just got through listening to Toller's conspiracy theories. He's a mean ruthless son of a bitch, but he's not politically stupid. When he gets on the media like he did today, he's got something more than hot air to back him up. Whatever it is, it connects with this business of Jonas'. And whatever it is, it's got Jonas scared shitless." Laurence turned and studied Tyler for a while. "You're scared, too. Not in quite the same way, but close." He brought his hands up, made a fist with one, and slapped it into the open palm of the other. "That much I know. And what I suspect," he continued, "is that Toller is right. There are others, more deaths Jonas is worried about. Deaths he thinks involve psy perceivers."

Tyler recalled her lecture to Jonas on the difference between inference and knowledge. She couldn't tell which of the two formed the basis for Laurence's guess, if that's what it was. But she could tell he was certain he was right.

Laurence waited, expecting some response from Tyler. But all he got back was the unrevealing blankness of her careful screening. "Tyler, tell me what this is all about." His words were as much a plea for trust as a demand for information.

Tyler's head bobbed in a gesture of frustration. "I can't."

"No, Tyler. You can. Maybe you won't. But you can." The feeling behind Laurence's words was cold, disdainful.

It caused a quick leap of anger within Tyler. "You know exactly the position I'm in."

"Yes, I know the position you're in." He gave pointed emphasis to his words. "Jonas' tame psy. What I'm telling you is you ought to stand with your own kind."

Through the whole conversation, Tyler had sorted a certain amount of contrivance in everything Laurence had said. A careful selection of word and response to provoke her. Not that he was insincere, but that he was, with calculation, using his sincerity to gain his end. But the last statement, if it had started as manipulation, carried a charge of emotional intensity that cut past Laurence's control. That emotion in Laurence demanded undivided loyalty, demanded an absolute acceptance of the need for choosing sides. Instinctively Tyler gave an inward gesture of rejection.

"You really hate that idea, don't you, Tyler?" Laurence persisted. "That we do need to define ourselves separately. Protect ourselves. Separately."

"The history of the world," Tyler said her own anger rising to meet his, "is strewn with the results of people defining themselves. Or being defined. Separately." She stretched out her arm and briefly laid her lighter skinned fingers on the back of his hand. "And you should understand that as well as anyone."

"I do," he said more quietly. "But it's never going to change. We...psy perceivers...are different. The rest of them know it." He gestured at the people walking by. "And we know it. What we've got to do is find some way to survive it. On our own terms. Not theirs."

There was a lifetime of conviction behind Laurence's words. Tyler had always known it, but she had never felt it so strong in him before. "That sounds like fanaticism," she said.

"Maybe it is," Laurence said sharply. "Just don't indulge yourself in being too judgmental. From the comfortable insulation of that country retreat of yours." For the moment, there was such contempt in Laurence that Tyler froze. But the contempt was followed by a flood of regret, not at the emotion itself but that so much of it had been revealed. "I'm sorry, Tyler." And he was, but the reality of the moment hung between them. "It's just...well, you *have* insulated yourself. And there are things I have to deal with, things I'm not about to leave to Jonas, to the government, to any non-psy. Things the League is not supposed to be involved with, officially."

"Officially, Laurence? You mean, legally."

"All the law allows me to do is run a giant PR machine," Laurence said derisively.

"So you disregard the law when you think it's necessary."

"Even you, Tyler, can't be that naive. Of course I do." Laurence's anger rose hot and undiluted. When it subsided, he added quietly, "I told you I'm not going to trust our welfare to Jonas or any other non-psy. No matter how well intentioned." Laurence sighed as if he had reached a decision. "We have...the League, I mean...I guess you'd call it an intelligence division. Illegal, yes. Among other things we keep tabs on, or try to, our political enemies. And that's not just people like Toller. It also includes the major anti-psy organizations, as well as the ebb and flow of the lunatic fringe."

As Laurence spoke, something connected for Tyler. She suddenly knew why he had recognized the name of the dead maintenance worker. "Willis Crayton. He was part of that lunatic fringe you're keeping under surveillance.

For a moment, Laurence withdrew, totally screened. But it was like a blink. Then he sighed again. "You caught my reaction, didn't you? When Jonas mentioned Crayton's name." Tyler nodded. Laurence glanced away and then looked back at her."Yeah. I'd heard of Willis Crayton before. You must have sorted I was glad when I heard the name. Glad he was dead. You tell Jonas that?"

"I told him you recognized the name. That's all."

"That's all?" Laurence gave a small rumble of distress. "That's enough to make me his prime suspect."

"Hardly that, but the point is if you and your private intelligence organization were keeping Crayton under surveillance, you must have had a reason, you must have known something about him." Laurence didn't respond. "I want you to tell me what you know," Tyler insisted.

"You see there's a problem with that, Tyler. I'm not so sure where my sympathies lie here. With the hunters, you, and Jonas, and Wilkins. Or with the hunted."

Tyler's skepticism was strong. "You can't mean that. If Crayton was murdered..."

Laurence interrupted. "People like Crayton, I wonder if you really have any idea. Talk about fanaticism, accuse me of it. You ought to experience some of their stuff sometime. Then tell me about the law. And about cooperating with due process." He frowned. "Maybe I've been too close to some of this for too long. All I know is, somebody like Crayton I'm glad he's dead. I didn't kill him, but I'm glad he's dead." It felt like the truth to Tyler. "And that is what Jonas is afraid of, isn't it? That Crayton was murdered, somehow, psyonically. By me. Or Dorian. Or somebody." This time it was Tyler who remained unresponsive. "If you want anything else from me," Laurence went on, "you're going to have to tell me what's going on. You're going to have to convince me that it's worth, maybe destroying the League."

Tyler thought for a while, trying to weigh the implications, especially the concerns Chief Wilkins had expressed about sharing information only the murderer could know. She knew Laurence had information too. She was also all but certain he wasn't going to give it up without sufficient reasons. If confiding in Laurence was a risk, it was a risk she decided she had to take.

"Over the last five months," she said, her voice calm, almost detached, "nine people have been found dead. Crayton was number ten. Apparently they all dropped dead in the street or some other public place, presumably of a stroke or brain hemorrhage. Only in every case, the prognosis for the likely cause of death was nonexistent. The probability that such cases would occur, given time span, proximity, other factors, well, the probability curve stands at nil right now. Statistically the deaths shouldn't have happened, but they did. Therefore the probability is that the deaths weren't natural, that someone caused them." Tyler could feel expectation and denial building in Laurence. "Only there is no known method by which the strokes or hemorrhages could have been induced." She allowed herself the slightest pause. "Except for a hypothetical possibility of psyonic impartment."

Laurence had anticipated what was coming and he burst out almost before Tyler had finished. "That's ridiculous." Denial flooded through him. "No one could do that. Use impartment that way."

"Data projections say it's theoretically possible," Tyler said evenly.

"I don't give a damn about their projections." Laurence's voice rose and one of the passersby glanced nervously in their direction.

Abruptly Tyler got up and said, "Let's walk." They strolled with deliberate casualness around the corner of the building where they had left the ceevee.

Chapter Seventeen

When they were alone, Laurence demanded hotly, "Do you have any idea how explosive even the suggestion of this could be?"

Frustration flared in Tyler. "Why do you think I'm helping Jonas? This thing's not going away. They get another death with no solution, no end in sight, Wilkins will have to go to Policy Commissioner Rackland. By all rights he should have already. And Rackland will take it straight to CBI. Then you can worry about consequences. To the League and the rest of us." She stared insistently at him. "Now tell me what you know."

Reluctance sat in Laurence like a stone. He took a couple of steps forward, and Tyler thought he was just going to walk off. But he stopped, reached into his jacket and pulled out his apps pad. He held it up for her to see. On its display was a list of eleven names. One of them was Willis Crayton, another was Joleson Randle. Eight of the others were familiar too. They matched the names on Jonas' list of questionable deaths. There was only one name she didn't recognize. Martin Bren.

Returning the apps pad to his jacket, Laurence said, "Any of yours on that list, besides Crayton?"

He knew the answer before she could reply, but Tyler nodded anyway. "Who are they?" she asked.

She could feel the hesitation in him, but at last he spoke. "You said it before. The lunatic fringe. Or a small part of it anyway." He leaned against the ceevee, head down, his arms folded. "Look, Tyler, the League keeps tabs on anti-psy activists. We infiltrate meetings, the

Protectors, the Guardians, those kinds of groups. We break the law about identifying ourselves. I even use some of us who've managed to evade registration." Catching her reaction, he added, "And yes, it's all highly illegal." Then slowly, with determination, he raised his head. "The men on that list, they're some kind of inner circle, formed around the one called Martin Bren. As far as we can tell, he seems to be the leader, the focus of this bunch. They'd turn up at meetings of the major anti-psy organizations. Never all at once, two or three at a time. But always Bren. And somehow in the course of the evening Bren would end up speaking. He's good at it."

"That's praise, coming from you."

"Spare me the onerous comparisons. Anyway, recently they just seemed to dry up. No more manipulated meetings, no more Bren. And frankly, we were just as glad." Laurence paused. "You're telling me they're all dead, the men on that list?"

Tyler nodded. "Except for Bren."

Laurence stood very still, his amazement not quite blotting out a strong sense of relief, even of gratification.

"Laurence." Tyler's voice was quiet, but underlying the quietness was a sense of shock.

Laurence's head jerked upward. His jaw tightened, his eyes were hot and angry. He made no effort to screen what he was feeling. "You want honesty from me, don't you?" he said defiantly. "Like Crayton, the people on my list, if they're dead, I have no tears for them. But I'll tell you something, this kind come and go all the time. They'll be plenty more to take their place. There'll always be the hate and hassle, the rabble rousing. But these," he slapped his hand against his jacket where he had tucked away his apps pad, "they weren't important, not important enough to kill. Any psy would know that."

"Even psy perceivers can act on emotion, at the expense of sense."

"You like to tell me how anyone could get something like that past the psychological profiles."

Tyler shrugged. "It could be an unregistered. Maybe even one of yours." She let an unspoken thought about his informants drift through her mind.

Laurence reacted to it immediately. "No. I won't turn anyone in. I won't betray the people who've trusted me." Before Tyler could argue with him, he went on, "I'll tell you what you should think about. It would make a lot more sense than imagining a psy crazy enough to risk bringing everything down around us. It's a set up. Maybe these ten *were* murdered. Sacrificed to the cause to provoke an anti-psy backlash. That motive would make a lot more sense."

"It's a nice theory. I even like it," Tyler said acidly. "There's only one difficulty. It doesn't deal with the problem of method."

"And I still say," Laurence insisted, "that's not the answer. Even to seriously consider impartment as a murder weapon, it's just part of the anti-psy prejudice which even your chums Jonas and Wilkins aren't entirely free of. As you well know. But I can't afford to be picky, not with Toller already involved in this. If he gets hold of the Stats and Prob report, he'll ride this all the way to a spate of laws that will make Riscoll look like a model of civil rights legislation. So I'll give you this. But not electronically." He reached into his jacket again and drew out a few pages of printout, folded lengthwise. "It's everything we've got on these people. It's not much. As I said, we didn't give them a very high priority, especially after they dropped out of sight." As he handed over the pages, Laurence added with a note of satisfaction, "The ink's unscannable."

"Cloak and dagger all the way," Tyler retorted. Then more mildly she said, "Wilkins will just have it all hand entered."

"I know. A minor inconvenience. And a reminder." Bitterness rose in Laurence. "I'm not happy about this. I'm not on the team."

Grateful but uneasy, Tyler took the pages. "Use your contacts to try to locate Bren. And reconsider about identifying, to Jonas at least, the unregistereds you've been using. You can't afford not to, Laurence. We...can't afford not to."

Laurence looked away, the strain he was feeling clearly visible on his face. "I'll do what I can about Bren. I've got to think about the other." Tyler knew it was pointless to press him. "You better make this worth it, Tyler. You, Jonas, and Wilkins. Because sharing even this much information is probably going to cost me the League. At least, the part of it that really matters." The spoken words had the flatness of an unnatural calm. Behind them raged Laurence's awareness of consequences and then a sudden regret at what he had just done.

"Come back and talk to Jonas," Tyler said.

"No. Let them find me, if they want me." He paused. "I haven't killed anyone, Tyler. And I'm damn sure nobody I've dealt with has either." Despite the deep ambivalence in Laurence, it seemed like the truth to Tyler. "But these eleven," he jabbed a finger at the pages of print out Tyler was holding, "if ten of them are dead, good riddance. And if someone is taking them out, I just hope he gets Bren too before you, Jonas, and the Chief track him down."

Tyler knew Laurence was ready to leave. It felt as if he wanted to walk away from his own ambiguity of feeling. But something was nagging at him, a last bit of information he was trying to make up his mind about. She could feel him come to a decision. "There's something else," he said. "You're not going to like it. And I don't see that it's any use. It's not exactly the kind of thing you're looking for." Tyler sorted a great distaste in Laurence, a distaste which encompassed her, himself, and the information he had. "We found out something else in our little espionage operation. Jonas' wife. For some time now, she's been attending anti-psy meetings. The Thought Protectors mostly, but a couple of the other groups too." Laurence shook his head in disgust. "I leave it to you to decide whether to tell Jonas." Then he turned and walked away, quickly but with no appearance of unusual urgency.

Tyler watched as Laurence made his way around the corner of the building and merged with the people strolling through the plaza, but she made no attempt to follow him. She was sure he had planned his departure as carefully as he had planned their arrival.

She looked with no great enthusiasm at the pages of printout Laurence had given her. If his information were correct, and she didn't doubt it, here at last was a connection between the victims. A handful of anti-psy activists. All dead in less than six months. If someone had targeted this particular group, they only had one to go. Martin Bren. Just how long would it be before he turned up dead? But even Bren's death would be no guarantee it was over. The murderer might just move on to a new set of targets. As Laurence had said, there would always be more like Bren and his cohorts. Wilkins would never be able to leave it at that. What was it he had said about leaving his city at risk? He wouldn't do that. He couldn't. They needed to know why these men were dead and they needed to know who was responsible. Now they had one possible victim left who might provide a link to the murderer. It didn't seem enough. In fact, it probably wasn't enough.

Chapter Eighteen

After Laurence left, an oppressive sense of inertia settled on Tyler. It was a mood compounded of futility, frustration, and maybe despair. It all added up to a feeling that this case Jonas had brought her would have disastrous consequences, no matter what the outcome. And that feeling was amplified by Laurence's news about Meryl Acre and her involvement with anti-psy groups. Somehow that information seemed an appropriately dismal emblem for this whole business. Eventually, Tyler knew, she would have to decide whether to tell Jonas. And when to tell him.

But Jonas' relationship with his wife, that concern was a luxury right now. Tyler forced herself to re-track, to abandon the allure of inaction. She called Jonas. "I've just seen Laurence," she began.

Jonas sputtered, "Where the hell is he?"

Tyler cut him off. "Listen. A man named Martin Bren," she spelled the name, "he's probably the next victim. Meet me back at Wilkins' office."

"Don't wait for that," Jonas said irritably. "Send the Chief whatever you've got. Now."

"Can't. Laurence only gave me printout. Scan blocked."

"That's just childish," Jonas exclaimed.

"Maybe. But Laurence liked it. So call Wilkins. Tell him about Bren. Tell him we're on our way." Tyler ended the call. She returned to the rental ceevee Laurence had left, programmed it for Enforcement headquarters and drove back into central metro. Jonas was already waiting in Wilkins' office when she arrived. As she shut the door, Jonas started to speak, "Tyler..." But she held up her hand, silencing him.

She crossed to Wilkins. Reaching over his desk, she handed him the pages of printout Laurence had given her. Wilkins took them. Sounding more amused than annoyed, he said, "I know. Can't scan these. Meredith's little stick in the eye. Jonas told me." He spread the pages out before him. Looking them over, he said smoothly, "Meredith and the League have been busy. But as far as Bren's concerned..." He touched his apps pad. On the wall panel behind him, the meager data that Enforcement had on Martin Bren appeared. Bold letters across the top of the display read, Inquiry: Martin Bren ID# 8Q9.453.2k7 Current whereabouts unknown. "As you see." Wilkins shrugged resignedly at Tyler.

Tyler made a grunt of discontent. Then she sat down and gave a selective account of her meeting with Laurence. Wilkins listened calmly, weighing the information she was giving him and wondering about what she was withholding.

But in Jonas there was a rising level of frustration. When she finished, he erupted. "That's just great. Laurence virtually refuses to cooperate. Provides himself with a motive at the same time." He looked at Tyler fiercely. "How could you just let him walk off?"

"Jonas." Chief Wilkins spoke over the outburst. More quietly, he said to Tyler, "Just tell me what you think."

"I think Laurence is telling the truth. He didn't murder Crayton, or anyone else."

"Despite the fact he's not sorry they're dead."

"That's right."

"How sure are you?" Wilkins asked, wanting the certainty he knew better than to expect.

Tyler shrugged. "I'm giving you my impression." She was consciously trying to repress her irritation, but her voice held an edge.

"Your impression," Jonas broke in again with unrestrained impatience. "That's a big help, isn't it?"

Tyler's anger bubbled over. She said bitingly, "If I recall, my impression is what you asked me for from the beginning."

Wilkins again tried for calm. "Jonas does understand that, at least he does when he's not quite so frustrated. Isn't that right, Jonas?"

Jonas nodded. "I'm sorry." He looked, and felt, chagrined.

"But Jonas is correct," Wilkins continued. "I'm not exactly used to taking someone's impression as evidence. But," he said before Tyler could respond, "it's a little different in this case. I suspect your impression is pretty reliable." Almost unwillingly, he added, "Still it's too bad you couldn't get Meredith to come in. If only for his own protection."

Tyler looked at the display. "In case this Martin Bren turns up dead."

"If that happened, we could have eliminated Meredith as a suspect," Wilkins said, his voice carefully neutral.

"I do assure you, Chief, I didn't need to point that out to him."

"No. I guess not."

Jonas stirred restlessly, his anger at Laurence barely controlled. "It's stupid. Laurence isn't accomplishing a damn thing by this and he knows it."

Wilkins' mouth twitched in a small gesture of dissent. "I suspect it's more than stubbornness on his part, Jonas. My guess is that Laurence Meredith has other tracks to cover than this bit of intelligence he's communicated to us. Such as, how he got it." Wilkins looked at Tyler inviting a response but she gazed back at him without comment. With a sigh, he drew together the scattered pages on his desk and stacked them. He handed them to Jonas, then turned to Tyler. "Of course, if you're right about Meredith, that does tend to direct our attention to D. Rath." He watched Tyler's expression. "I have put out another interrogatory. She and her lawyer are on their way over here now."

Wilkins turned back to the display. He rapidly scrolled through Enforcement's information on Martin Bren. "Well, Bren's a case," he said. "No permanent address, not for years. No comm provider account. Contact through a variety of drop boxes. Employment sporadic. No police record. No tax complaints. The last time anyone kept track of him was fifteen years ago when he did his two years of Civic Service. Worked in non-technical maintenance." Wilkins raised his eyebrows. "And it looks like we'll have to take Meredith's word about Bren's anti-psy activities. He's not on any membership lists, at least, nothing *we've* got on record."

Jonas looked up from Laurence's pages to the display of Enforcement's official data on Bren. Tyler felt the first glimmer of relief in him. "You really think this is it? That Bren's intended to be the next victim?"

Wilkins gestured noncommittally. "If we can assume Meredith's information is reliable, I'd say that's right."

"Still, this Bren and the rest of them," Jonas tapped the pages of Laurence's report against his knee, "they seem so...inconsequential. Of all the crazies loose in metro, why these?" Jonas had directed his question to the air, not expecting an answer.

"Laurence wonders about that, too," Tyler said. After a moment, she added thoughtfully, "Bren's as close to a cipher as you can be today, isn't he?"

Wilkins glanced at her and nodded. He took back from Jonas the pages of printout and leafed through them. Finally he said, "This may explain why Bren's still alive. The rest of them had permanent addresses or permanent employment. Even comm accounts in some cases. Makes them easier to locate. But we'll find Bren, we've got the resources." Tyler could feel the Chief's certain confidence in the world he commanded. He believed his law enforcement operations, once enlisted to track down Martin Bren, would do so with efficiency. "Now that we know who we're looking for, we'll find him," he repeated.

"Then what?" Tyler asked.

Wilkins' usually bland expression remained unchanged except for a tightening around the eyes. "That's what we'll have to decide." His stare tightened still more. "Bait or protective custody, that's going to be the call, isn't it?"

Jonas broke in. "You pull him in and he is supposed to be the last victim, we may never get the killer."

Wilkins continued to watch Tyler. "If the things we've hypothesized are true, do you think we could protect Bren? On the street, I mean."

Tyler knew the question, or more precisely the expectation of her answer, provoked anxiety in Jonas. "I doubt it," she said. "We don't know enough about what we're dealing with." Wilkins looked at her inquisitively, the desire for further explanation strong in him. He didn't bother to put his inquiry into words. Tyler went on, "I don't know how fast one of...us...could sort what was happening. And I don't know if we could stop it."

"What do you think?"

Tyler got up and walked to the window. She stood looking down at the mass of the metro sprawled below her. She turned back to face Wilkins and Jonas. Haloed by the light from the window, her face was indistinct. "I think, if this killer is an unregistered CF4 who's been able to remain unidentified, and who has sufficient control of impartment to use it to kill people," she took a noticeable breath, "then I think, whoever it is can do what they damn well want, and none of us, other psy perceivers, I mean, could stop it."

She didn't bother to sort the muddle of emotion in Jonas and Wilkins, but she knew it was compounded largely of anxiety and indecisiveness.

After a while, she could feel the Chief forcibly turn his attention. "Well, we have to find Bren first. When we do, his actions are going to influence whatever plans we make." Wilkins reviewed the material on Bren in Laurence's report. "According to what Meredith's been able to get, Bren doesn't just hate psy perceivers, he doesn't trust anyone. Government officials and police at the head of the list." His lips twitched but didn't quite make it to a grim smile. "Thinks we're all in league with the psy menace."

"According to his view of things, you are," Tyler said. She was still at the window, perched, half-sitting, half-standing, against the narrow ledge. She noticed Wilkins watching her. It was the gaze of a professional observer, but she sorted a trace of sympathy in him as well.

"I can't promise anything about the League," he said.

Tyler looked at him with bleak amusement. "You see, Chief Wilkins, you don't have to be psy to sense what people are feeling."

"Tyler," Wilkins said emphatically, "I've got two priorities. The first is to get this killer off the streets. I'll sacrifice anything to achieving that. The second is trying to help Jonas keep this as quiet as possible. I'll do my best with that one. But at the end of this, if we can bring it to an end, I'm going to have to do some tradeoffs, maybe some with the letter of the law, and certainly some with Hardin Toller." Wilkins shifted uneasily. "As for the League and its unauthorized information gathering," he ran the words together derisively, "that may have to be the bone I throw to our esteemed legislator to distract him from the real meat. You understand what I'm saying."

"I understand you." Tyler could feel her patience draining away. The sense of futility which she had carried away from the meeting with Laurence persisted and strengthened. She could not conjure in herself any faith in their collective ability to meet both of Wilkins' priorities. She was glad they could not actually feel her mood, although she knew the Chief had read her pretty well.

She pushed herself away from the window ledge. "I'm tired. You need me for anything else right now?"

"No," Jonas said. "You going back to the hotel?"

She nodded and started for the door.

Wilkins' voice stopped her. "I want you to know. If we can pin this down, find out who's responsible for these deaths, I will try to find a way to keep these murders under wraps. I told that to Jonas from the beginning. But we've got to get the killer. The one thing I won't do, I can't do, is leave this open-ended, wondering when it will all start again." He allowed more fervor in his voice than he had previously.

Tyler knew he meant it, and he wanted her to know it, to believe it, too. "Yes. I know you'll try." But she sounded as unconvinced as she felt.

Without waiting for anything more, Tyler opened the door to the outer office to find herself confronting a tall, angular man. He appeared poised to charge the doorway where she stood. Positioned beside him was an officer who managed to look both authoritative and diplomatic. Behind them, flanked by a couple of additional enforcement people, and looking a familiar blend of alertness and detachment, was Dorian Rath.

It took the artful grouping a second or two to come alive, but when it did the tall man bustled past Tyler into the Chief's office, the enforcement officer at his heels. The door shut behind them.

Tyler sorted from Dorian a flicker of mock irritation, a carefully assumed semblance of the genuine feeling it was intended to disguise.

Tyler turned her head slightly toward the door behind her. "Your lawyer." It was a statement, not a question.

"Yes," Dorian said. "He was a little impatient at having to wait while the major players finished their business."

"Unlike you?"

"It's not so much my patience as my curiosity that's being tried." Dorian paused, and then added, "Of late." She smiled blandly. "Of course, Chief Wilkins is helping a little. No more volunteered statements. Full and official interrogatory this time."

"I know," Tyler said, and she could hear the defensiveness in her own voice.

"So they really do think the little janitor was killed. And somehow I suspect their reaction is more than just officialdom's fear of Hardin Toller." Dorian's voice had grown sharper. She stared past Tyler at the closed door. She was screening carefully, but Tyler needed no psy ability to know Dorian was reviewing everything she knew and everything she guessed.

Dorian switched her gaze from the door back to Tyler. And then allowed what appeared to be genuine bewilderment to surface. "They think they've got a murder, maybe a series of murders, if the honorable legislator is to be believed. And they're really focusing on Laurence and me? Tyler, what in the hell have you been telling them?"

As far as Tyler could determine, there was no posing in Dorian at all, but nonetheless all Tyler returned to her was blankness.

Dorian's mood held for a moment and Tyler braced herself for another appeal for candor. Dorian caught the reaction. Whatever her original intention might have been, Dorian withdrew again behind her own careful defenses. She smiled brittlely and said, "Whatever you told Jonas after the reception obviously didn't let *me* off the hook any more than it did Laurence."

She started past Tyler to follow her lawyer into Wilkins' office. With a hand on the door, she stopped. She gave Tyler a full stare and very carefully thought out the words, *so it's not just something to do with impartment, but murder, murder by psy impartment...messy, very messy.*

She continued on into the office, shutting the door behind her.

Kaslan, Decker, Revella, et. al. *Current Psyonics: Research in Progress* (Summary) Grant #1001-PSY-1242-K5. Government Distribution Office. <gdo.gov> March 2038. Open Access. (See File Psy-1242-000 for complete text, data, and documentation.)

The first suspected cases of genuine psyonic capability appeared and were documented during sensory deprivation experiments conducted in the 1990s. The psy factor in brain activity was conclusively identified by Haskins during his classic experiments conducted during the period 2016-2019. (See complete text for details of the period 1990-2020.)

Psyonic capability consists of three distinct elements: perception, sorting, and impartment. Although to some degree we can discuss these separately, the interrelationship between these elements must always be borne in mind. Particularly we must remember that the effective use of psy function depends on the ability to integrate the first two of these elements.

1. Perception: The base of all psy function is perception, the ability to sense the generalized state of consciousness experienced by others. Under normal circumstances this undifferentiated aware state, termed the constant, consists of a continuous flow of disorganized emotional, imagistic, and ideational content. At the level of simple perception, the constant is too chaotic to furnish any meaningful sensory data. It is a random and constantly fluctuating body of input. Analogies between psy function and the other senses are always potentially misleading. Still elemental psy perception of another's constant might be likened to the visual experience of watching a steadily and rapidly rotating kaleidoscope.

The first and most obvious control factor (CF) for psy function is closure, that is the ability to shut out psy perception. Again to use a visual metaphor, closure is the rough equivalent of shutting one's eyes. For psy perceivers (this designation is considered less connotative than and therefore preferable to telepath) closure marks the first great division in control over psy function. The PsyCF0 lacks the capacity for closure. For the CF0, psy function is truly a devastating personal burden. CF0s find themselves subjected to a barrage of sensory input which they can neither blot out nor render coherent. Many are driven into mental disorders by this overlay of shapeless and constant sensory stimuli. Almost total isolation or seclusion is the only relief these unfortunates can find.

Various research projects have investigated the possibility of eradicating psy perception. None have been successful. The effects of drugs, including narcotics and hallucinogens, have been shown to be very erratic, varying greatly with the individual. In some cases they distort psy perception, in others they appear to have little, if any, effect. Resonance imaging has failed to disclose any specific areas of the brain which could be manipulated to interfere with psy perception or extirpated to eliminate it. It does appear that, like other sensory operations, psy perception is non-operative in an unconscious individual, although research in this area is by no means definitive.

In contrast to the Psy CF0, the psy perceiver with a CF1 rating has the capability for closure. In fact, the average CF1 functions in a state of closure most of the time. Without significant sorting ability (see discussion below), the CF1 finds little beneficial use for psy function. Preliminary studies indicate that a CF1 psy perceiver learns very early (probably by age 3 or 4) to accept closure as the normal state of psy perception. In these cases, psy function is shut out 70-80% of the time. Studies indicate that these are normal levels of closure for this rating. The higher the psy rating, the smaller the percentage of time spent in closure. Typically, a CF4 spends less than 10% of waking hours in closure. There are no cases on record of a psy perceiver at any CF level who maintains closure as a permanent state.

A CF1 may be characterized as a person given to flashes of intuition. These, of course, are simply the result of the occasional usable bit of psy perception. These will occur if the individual who is being perceived is experiencing a dominant emotional or ideational state. Such a dominant state will emerge from the undifferentiated whole of the constant and be perceivable by a CF1. It should be noted that dominant emotional states provide the simplest and most accessible material for psy perception. To sort even short verbal formulations requires a more complex application of psy function. (Further study is needed to determine the degree to which PsyCF1 'pick up' or sort images.)

2. Sorting: As we have already seen, the usefulness of psy perception is determined by the second element of psy function which is the sorting capability, that is the ability to order the constant, the raw material of psy perception, into meaningful sensory data. Only to the extent that psy perception can be ordered does it become something of practical use to the psy perceiver. Thus it is only when we arrive at a CF2 capability that we begin to consider the psy perceiver as possessing a significant psy capability. It is suspected, although heretofore unproven, that sorting is a more sophisticated form of closure in which psy perception is not totally suppressed but is somehow adjusted at an ongoing rate. CF2 perceivers demonstrate a range of sorting ability. At the lowest end of the range are psy perceivers whose ordering of the sensory input might be compared to radio reception overlaid with static. At the higher end of the range, the CF2 can, with concentration, maintain a fairly steady coherence in the perception of another's constant.

In addition to the use of sorting to order psy perception, another component holds particular significance for telepathic communication between psy perceivers. That is the screening ability. In general CF2s lack screening ability to any significant degree. That is they are unable to consistently mask content from their own constant in the presence of another psy perceiver.

Only with the rating of CF3 do we arrive at reasonably good screening ability. All CF3s have fairly good control at blocking the perception of their own constant by another psy perceiver. The CF3 screening capability always occurs in combination with high range sorting ability. The typical CF3 comes reasonably close to the old and grossly inaccurate concept of psy perceivers as mind readers. The CF3 has a sorting capacity which functions very naturally and provides ongoing coherent sensory impressions, primarily of the dominant emotional states of the people around them. In most instances, the CF3 can also sort images and any unspoken verbalizations which have formed in the mind of the person being perceived. The screening ability of CF3s tends to be very effective. However, it may break under conditions of extreme stress or it may be countered by the higher level sorting ability of a CF4.

3. Impartment: As sorting is thought to be a more sophisticated form of closure, so impartment is thought to be a more sophisticated form of sorting. This interlocking relationship between the three elements of psy function remains theoretical, but, at the very least, may provide a useful framework for the integration of the elements of psy function. Impartment is the least known, and potentially the most controversial, element of psy function. If sorting can be likened to reception, impartment is the analogic equivalent of transmission, of sending the psy impulse. The capacity for impartment which carries with it a rating of CF4 is evident only in psy perceivers who already demonstrate all CF3 capabilities. CF4s exhibit very high range control over all previously discussed psy capabilities. They not only have excellent control over the sorting or ordering of psy perception, they are also very skillful at screening or controlling the degree of psy perception which can be practiced upon them. This combination of very high ordering ability with very skillful screening ability is common to all CF4s.

However the true hallmark of the PsyCF4 is the capacity for impartment. CF4s can with great concentration and, as far as can be judged, with great expenditure of energy actually 'plant' articulated words in someone else's consciousness. No CF4 on record does this casually because of the tremendous mental effort which true impartment seems to demand.

Of further interest is the fine distinction between 'normal' psy communication and actual impartment. Psy perceivers of CF2 rating or above can use unspoken verbal formulations to communicate. But this is a case of high level reception and sorting, not of impartment. For example, a psy perceiver can deliberately 'think' a word or sentence and have that unspoken verbalization be sorted by another psy perceiver. Impartment, on the other hand, is the ability to actively force an unspoken verbalization into the mind of another.

Initial incidents of impartment appear to be inadvertent, usually occurring in childhood, often at moments of emotional stress. CF4s in the highest ranges demonstrate a limited ability to achieve impartment at will.

Controlled impartment has been attempted under experimental conditions both with two psy perceivers and with a psy perceiver and a conventional perceiver. Psy perceivers have described being on the receiving end of impartment in a variety of ways. Lower range psy perceivers have found the experience disquieting. They report discomfort at being unable to shut out or 'turn off' imparted words. Higher range psy perceivers, CF3s and other CF4s, tend to report the experience as interesting and do not seem to consider it as threatening as do lower range psy perceivers. Because of the apparent inability of psy perceivers to maintain impartment for any extended period, no data is available on the potential for one CF4 to block or close against the impartment ability of another.

Of significant interest is the great distress shown by conventional perceivers subjected to impartment. They report finding the experience very frightening. "As if I was thinking someone else's thoughts...as if someone else had taken over my mind" were typical comments. These subjective reactions are supported by changes in involuntary physiological functions, such as increase in blood pressure, heart rate, and other typical reactions that mark physical response to stress. Since impartment, at least in theory, would allow unspoken communication between a psy perceiver and a non-psy, additional research is necessary to determine if these extremely negative reactions can be overcome.

The possibility of a psy perceiver with a fully developed CF4 functionality must be considered. Such a psy perceiver would demonstrate a comprehensive range of impartment ability, including the impartment not only of words but of images and emotional states. Probability studies based on experiments done thus far give some indication that extended application of impartment, particularly of images and emotional states, could be employed to induce serious psychological or physiological stress in the recipient, perhaps even to lethal levels. Hypothetical projections of increases in blood pressure, heart rate, etc. which might result from the sustained reception of impartment suggest that, theoretically at least, this element of psy function could have dangerous consequences for anyone subjected to it. However it must be emphasized that no such level of impartment has ever been recorded. The current state of research indicates that the degree of energy necessary to create even brief occurrences of impartment appears to provide a natural limit on the functioning of this capability. To employ a simple image, it is hypothesized that the levels of energy necessary to achieve impartment which could result in physical harm to the recipient are so high they would literally 'burn out' the psy perceiver who attempted to use them. For this reason, the CF4 with the ability to impart single words, phrases, and short sentences probably marks the limit of psy function.

In closing it is interesting to note that, as we move from perception to impartment, the roles of the basic mental states within the constant reverse. With regard to the sorting function, it is emotional states which are most readily perceived and ordered by the psy perceiver. In contrast, the ability to sort words out of the constant indicates very high range psy ability. Thus it is CF3 and CF4 psy perceivers who can most easily 'read' unspoken verbalizations. However, in the case of impartment, the 'sending' of unspoken verbalizations appears to be the starting point of that function. It is probably also the ending point. To date, the only recorded cases of impartment are the 'sending' of such unspoken verbalizations. There are no recorded cases of a psy perceiver imparting emotional states or imagery. At present, the possibility of such impartment remains hypothetical.

Chapter Nineteen

Tyler lay sprawled on the sofa. A cup of coffee sitting on the floor beside her had grown cold. Since her meeting two days ago with Jonas and Chief Wilkins to share Laurence's information, she had kept to her hotel suite, hoping to find the familiar comfort in solitude, but all she had found was a sense of oppression that weighed increasingly upon her. And none of the feeble activities of yesterday and today had lightened the burden one bit.

Intermittently she had tried to work on the chapters she had brought with her, but the revisions she attempted failed to satisfy her, each rewrite seeming clumsier than the one before it. She had heard from Jonas a couple of times with reports on their efforts to locate Bren. They were trying to run down any possible haunts of his and had a few leads, but nothing definite yet. The Chief's confidence notwithstanding, Tyler doubted they'd find Bren at all. Ten people he'd associated with were dead, and he'd probably long gone to ground. But Jonas had reported that the Chief had another opinion. Wilkins was convinced Bren would never capitulate completely to whatever fears he might have. That his obsessive sense of mission would force him to surface eventually. Of course, it was all speculation, based on Wilkins' reading of Laurence's information, which was sketchy enough.

Tyler had also called Dorian to ask how things had gone for her with Wilkins. "I'm under an interrogatory, so IsogaCorp will have to wait," Dorian had said. Then added, "It's a little late for you to be worrying about consequences, isn't it? What's the matter, finding your role uncomfortable?" Tyler hadn't bothered to remind her that she had found it uncomfortable from the beginning. Dorian knew that anyway. Dorian had continued, "The only reason I'm not in custody is they figure there's more to be gained by giving me a little rope. See if I'll incriminate myself. Or someone else." She had given a mutter of impatience. "Do they really think I'm stupid enough not to know I'm being watched?" Dorian hadn't waited for an answer, but had closed out the call.

Undoubtedly Dorian was right, Tyler had thought. Enforcement must have her under surveillance. With just an interrogatory they couldn't require her to wear a tracking instrument. Still, as long as Dorian's comm was on, they could locate her if necessary. But Tyler guessed they were probably keeping her under direct observation as well.

Through it all, Tyler's gloom persisted. Finally late in the afternoon she had accepted what was really bothering her. She had spent most of the last day and a half thinking not about the possibility of murder by impartment but about Meryl Acre. About Meryl Acre, Jonas' wife, who attended anti-psy meetings. What was it she had said at the reception? "I don't mean anything against you people, but I wish he'd resign." Tyler had put it down to worry over Jonas' recent preoccupations, but it was obvious Meryl Acre's resentment went much deeper than that. Tyler still didn't know what to do about it. Whether to tell Jonas, and more than anything, how to tell him.

So this day had wound its way to an unprofitable end. The one thought Tyler wanted to concentrate on seemed unable to make its way out of the jumble of her conflicting concerns. The recollection she wanted, that moment of fleeting perception in the lobby the night of Crayton's death, remained elusive. And the more time went by, the less likely it seemed possible to recapture it from her accumulation of mental debris and physical lethargy.

For now, there seemed to be nothing more she could do about Bren, or Dorian for that matter, but the problem Laurence had dumped on her, maybe she could take a little charge of that. She took her apps pad and searched for a phone number for Meryl Acre but all she found was a website for "MA Software Consulting." It had a contact link but what she had to say she wasn't going to put in an email.

Tyler thought for a moment, then using the private number he'd given her, she called Chief Wilkins. She could hear the surprise in his voice. "Tyler. Jonas was supposed to call you," he said.

"He did." Tyler hesitated. She knew she was interrupting him when he wanted all his attention on the search for Bren. "Look, I know you're in the middle of things, but I need something from you."

"Are you all right?" he asked.

"Yes. It's nothing to do with...this business. It's a personal matter. I want to reach Jonas' wife and I don't want him to know. Can you get me a number for her?"

Wilkins said, "Tyler, are you sure there isn't something...?"

"I'm just wondering if you know how I can reach Meryl Acre privately."

There was a brief silence before the Chief answered, "Yeah, wait a second." After a pause he read off a number, then added, "She's does IT. Free lance. Debugs programs. Pretty good at it I understand. Jonas has mentioned she's in the middle of a big project. Been keeping her pretty busy. Taking up most of her evenings. She might not pick up."

"She can call me back," Tyler said.

"You sure you don't want to tell me what this is about?" Wilkins asked.

"No. I told you, it's just something I want to talk to her about."

As Tyler entered the number Wilkins had given her, she wondered how many of those late evenings Meryl Acre had spent not working but with the Thought Protectors. When the call went through, she got the message system. "Meryl Acre here. Leave your name and number. I'll call when I can."

"This is Tyler West. I'd very much like to speak with you. My number..."

Meryl Acre's voice broke in. "T. West. Yes, I'm here. Is it something about Jonas?"

"No," Tyler said quickly, reassuringly. "It's a...I'd like to see you. As soon as it's convenient."

"See me? Why?" Meryl Acre sounded surprised and not entirely pleased.

In the awkwardness of the moment, Tyler began to regret her impulsiveness.

"There's something I'd like to discuss with you," Tyler said, realizing as she said it that she'd need to invent some credible excuse.

"Can't you tell me over the phone?"

Tyler wondered if she imagined the antagonism she sensed in Meryl Acre, the obvious unwillingness to meet. "It's just something I'd rather discuss in person."

"Is that so you can use," Meryl Acre hesitated over her choice of words, "your special abilities while you're talking to me?"

That was much too uncomfortably close to the truth because Tyler had no intention of confronting Meryl Acre directly about the Thought Protectors. But she hoped to sort some reaction from her, something which would help her decide what to do. Still outright denial would be pointless. Tyler decided on limited honesty.

"I guess I'm always more comfortable when I can use a full range of perception."

"You're being very mysterious about this, you know." Meryl Acre sounded just a bit hectoring.

"I'm sorry. I don't mean to be." Tyler decided to shift the burden of reaction. "Look, if meeting with me makes you uncomfortable..."

"No." The reversal was quick. "It's just...I'm awfully pressed for time. Still I'll be finishing for the evening soon. I'll stop by, if that's all right. You're at the Park Plaza, aren't you?" Tyler confirmed it. Meryl Acre added, her voice friendlier than it had been, "Jonas says he always gets you as close to the greenery as he can when you come into the city. Anyway it'll be about an hour."

The hour passed, but Meryl Acre didn't arrive. Tyler tried her number again, but this time no one interrupted the voice message. She had no sooner hung up than her own phone beeped. She was sure it was Meryl Acre explaining the delay. But it wasn't, it was Laurence.

He didn't bother with any preliminaries. "I've got a line on Bren. Reasonably reliable information he'll be in the 300 block of Birch Street, sometime late tonight. Word is, he's used one of the old storefronts along there as a safe house in the past. Your buddies," Laurence bit the word off sharply, "might try a stakeout."

It all meant of course that Laurence's spy operation was still in business. Tyler understood that. But all she said was, "All right. I'll tell them."

Laurence paused. "What are Jonas and Wilkins going to do with Bren if they find him?"

"Try to get him to accept some kind of protective custody, I suppose. Till they can figure out what to do next."

"Helping to rescue Martin Bren gives me no satisfaction." Laurence's voice glinted with anger.

"Laurence, go to Jonas."

"I'll come in when I'm ready." He ended the call.

Tyler called Wilkins immediately. When he answered, he sounded more harried than he had earlier, impatient with another interruption. As Laurence had done with her, Tyler spoke without preamble. "Martin Bren is supposed to turn up in the 300 block of Birch Street later tonight."

There was a full moment of silence from the Chief. "Where'd this come from?" Without waiting, he answered his own question. "Meredith?"

"He just called."

"That's all he said?"

"He said he had reasonably reliable information Bren might return to a safe house he's used there before."

"Reasonably reliable. Is that what he calls it?" Tyler kept silent. "I'm sorry," Wilkins said. "I don't like being forced to use what I don't approve of. But beggars can't be choosers. Thank him for me, if you get a chance."

"I doubt I will."

"Anyway, like it or not, I hope he's right. We'll check it out." Then before Tyler could end the call, Wilkins continued, "I wanted you to know. We're going to try to bring Bren in. I don't think we can protect him otherwise."

"That's what I expected."

"We'll get this killer, Tyler." When Tyler didn't respond, Wilkins said, "Anyway, thanks." She couldn't tell if he sounded apologetic or defensive.

After her conversation with Chief Wilkins, Tyler felt increasingly restless. She knew it was in part a discontent with waiting while others acted. After a while, even though no second call had come in during her conversations with Laurence and Wilkins, she tried Meryl Acre again. Got the message again and no other response. She wondered if Meryl Acre would avoid seeing her indefinitely. At least, it seemed she wasn't going to keep her appointment tonight. It was after eleven, almost two hours since they'd talked.

Tyler walked out onto the balcony. The day had been hot and muggy, but a quick summer storm was moving in. It was still warm, but the wind had come up, driving clouds across a moon that was almost full. The trees below, intermittently visible, were alive with the sound of thrashing leaves.

Suddenly Tyler could no longer stand the confinement of her rooms. They had ceased to be a refuge. Instead all the frustrations and uncertainties of the last few days seemed to have concentrated within their walls. Only the turbulence of the wind and the promise of rain seemed to offer relief.

Abruptly Tyler strode back inside, grabbed a raincoat, and went down to the park. The lights of the security kiosk seemed to wink amid the wind blown branches. But even without that reminder of protection, the park at night would have held no fear for her. She would know if anyone were near, but now in the approaching storm, the park appeared deserted.

The wind tore at the leaves overhead and the air was heavy with moisture but there was no rain yet. The clouds chased each other across the moon, causing its light to flicker from bright shine to full darkness. She followed the path to the center of the park, sought out her familiar bench and sat to watch the storm gather. In the fleeting passes of moonlight, the monument and the benches seemed alive with movement.

She was aware of the faint murmur of perception which always accompanied her, but as always, here, she felt satisfactorily remote from the city around her.

She thought for a while about Meryl Acre and why she had not shown up. Maybe something had come up with her work. And maybe it wasn't such a good idea to use a meeting with her as a way to try to decide what and whether to tell Jonas about his wife's interest in anti-psy fringe groups. Maybe it wasn't really any of her business at all. Her business was trying to help Jonas and Wilkins find a killer. A hypothetical psyonic killer. Tyler stopped and considered the first adjective. Did she really still believe the possibility of using impartment as a weapon was only hypothetical? Unhappily she had to admit that possibility no longer seemed as remote as she would have liked it to be.

She pushed aside that gloomy acknowledgment and reminded herself, actually her business was writing books and it was about time she got back to it. After all Jonas had never issued a Demand. She hadn't forced him to. That meant she could leave any time. The thought held overwhelming temptation. Now there was a good chance Jonas would accept her decision even if she did leave. After all, she had helped somewhat. They knew Bren was probably next on the list. That was something. And thanks to Laurence, there was a good chance they'd locate him tonight. If she really wanted, tomorrow morning, she could be home.

Tyler came out of her reverie, disquieted, without knowing why. She focused her attention outward as if she expected to sense the presence of someone else, someone who had come into her range of perception, but nothing seemed to have changed. The only presence with her was the wind which had risen even more. Still her thoughts had momentarily felt alien to her.

Tyler shook off the distraction. More realistically, she would go home not tomorrow, but probably soon. Because there didn't seem to be much else she could offer. Not unless she could dredge out that recalcitrant bit of perception she had sorted in the aftermath of Crayton's death. But she had replayed those moments in her mind too often. Her recollection of the scene was too automatic. The images, the impressions, were set and there seemed to be no room for anything new. She and Dorian waiting, carefully closed against each other. Cal Houlston shepherding Laurence. Jonas standing in the background with his wife. Someone else, she thought for a moment. Yes, Doug Selnik waiting to leave. Somewhere in that scene a scattered bit of reaction had momentarily slipped past someone's screening. But whose it might have been or what it might have meant continued to elude her.

Tyler sighed, leaned back, and stretched out her legs. The air was growing heavier and she watched distant gleams of lightning. They were still too far away to bring the sound of thunder but she decided it was time to go back to the hotel and try to sleep. She stood up. Maybe they'd get Bren tonight. Maybe Jonas would decide there wasn't anything more she could do. She shifted her weight as she prepared to walk away, but she never took the step. She froze.

Chapter Twenty

With a chill of apprehension, Tyler realized someone had come near, someone who could not be a conventional perceiver. Someone who had screened their presence as only another psy perceiver could — screen. Someone she had almost missed, except that a couple of minutes ago the careful screening had failed for a glimmering moment. She had dismissed it then, but not this time.

A murmur of words answered her thought. "No. Not this time."

Certainty formed in Tyler and with it an uncanny sense that an inevitable confrontation had finally arrived. Then Tyler heard her name, but this time the voice she heard spoke only in her mind.

--Tyler.--

With the impartment of her name came regret, a strange prophetic sorrow for a loss that had not yet happened. In a meeting of thought and instinct, Tyler felt the impulse to run, but somewhere between brain and muscle the impulse died.

The unspoken voice sounded again.

--Tyler.--

The word formed within her with the same mournful note of sorrow and regret. And Tyler felt afraid because the sorrow and regret were for her.

Tyler did not screen her fear but left it open for the other to sort. Whoever it was stood hidden somewhere in the darkness of the trees beyond the circle. The other's presence was familiar, but not yet identifiable. Tyler strained to sort something herself, but the other's screening was too good.

Tyler knew her heart was beating faster and that she was sweating. "You here to kill me?" she said aloud to the darkness. Even to herself, her voice sounded high and tinny.

The other ignored the question and asked soundlessly, --Why tonight, Tyler? Why do you think they might find Martin Bren tonight?--

The other's impartment seemed effortless to Tyler, writing the words across her mind at will, leaving her feeling strangely disconnected from herself. The world outside of herself, the wind, the turmoil of trees, the driven clouds, seemed even more remote.

--You *were* thinking about Bren. Where is he, Tyler? Tell me where he is?--

Tyler could not shut out the insinuating voice in her head, the words which were insistently her own, yet not her own. She struggled for control over her awareness, to screen her own knowledge, but it became increasingly difficult to separate herself from the other.

--Is it that important to you to protect Martin Bren, Bren and his band of hate? Where is he, Tyler?--

Tyler rasped a sharp intake of breath. "Give this up," she choked out.

--Not until I finish what I've started. And I will finish it.--

Sudden shattering recognition, bright as lightning, flared in Tyler and she knew. In that knowledge, she found her voice again. "Meryl Acre. My God. Meryl."

A shadow detached itself from one of the trees and Meryl Acre stepped out into the fitful moonlight. Her face was pale and indistinct, her eyes were blank, dark pools. When she finally spoke out loud again, her voice was incongruously matter-of-fact. "I only came to figure out what to do about your call. Needless to say, I wasn't really anxious to risk another face to face with you. Our meeting at the reception was quite enough, enough for me to confirm how well Jonas had chosen. Not that I really had any doubts about that." She paused. "Still that evening I felt I needed to take your measure."

Tyler stiffened. "Not only that," she said, her understanding falling into place.

Meryl Acre stepped closer. "Well, I thought you should have a good reason for any anxiety I might not be able to screen from you. Just in case I couldn't avoid you completely."

"The concerned wife," Tyler snapped.

"A genuine role is the easiest to play."

"And in the lobby that evening..." Tyler's comprehension of that moment which had eluded her for so long now seemed obvious to her. "It was you. Your sense of triumph. And you knew I'd sorted it. So you used impartment to redirect my awareness. Away from what momentarily slipped past your screening." Meryl Acre moved her head slightly in a gesture of agreement. "I should have known," Tyler said bitterly. "It kept nagging at me."

"You had no way of knowing anyone could use impartment the way I can." Meryl Acre said it simply, without arrogance. "Anyway, tonight I decided to come over and wait for you. I figured when I didn't show, there was a good chance you'd come out here for a while." The uncertain light blurred Meryl Acre's face, but Tyler knew she smiled. "I decided it was time I did a little discreet spying of my own, see if I could find out what you called about without you knowing. And I did. It's nice of you to be so concerned about Jonas' feelings, worrying about his wife's anti-psy involvement.

"But I got considerably more than I bargained for. Or at least I will have, when you tell me where Martin Bren is. It amazes me how elusive he's been. But then I guess paranoia has its uses. Although that's not exactly fair, since the danger he fears is real. Then again, so is the danger he poses. So tell me where he is, Tyler."

Denial washed out of Tyler in great waves, not just denial of the information Meryl Acre wanted, but of the irrevocability of what Meryl Acre had already done. Ten people dead and now Meryl Acre stood before her with the implacable will to kill another. An outburst of anger and frustration flamed through Tyler. She drew strength from the rage within her. Slowly and with exhausting concentration, she took her own words into Meryl Acre's consciousness.

--Meryl. Hear me. What you are saying is...insane. Give this up. Give this up now.--

It was the most extended impartment Tyler had ever attempted. The effort it took seemed a mockery against the ease of the other's ability. But Meryl Acre responded with surprise and a strange satisfaction. Underlying both, like an aftertaste, was bitterness.

--You surprise me. I imagine you surprise yourself. You could be very good. Maybe as good at impartment as I am.--

With dull weariness, Tyler said, "To what end, Meryl?"

--That would be your choice.--

Tyler summoned her remaining energy and fusing it with all the disgust she felt, imparted the one word.

--Murder?--

--Self-defense,-- Meryl countered. The words filled Tyler's mind like an echo of her own thought. --The idea revolts you doesn't it. I think you once said something to Jonas about it being difficult to ignore what you know. That's true. I can't ignore what I know.--

"Just what is it you think you know?" Tyler had to force her words out, past the ones with which Meryl Acre so effortlessly filled her head.

--First you need to know Martin Bren.--

Imperceptibly Tyler's grasp of the separation between herself and the voice in her head dissolved again, replaced by a clamor, a clamor of many voices. The voices must have been her because there was no one else for them to be. And yet they weren't. All at once, a leader. And a crowd responding. And they must have been her too because there was no one else. There was only a flux of thought and feeling. And that thought and feeling must have been her too. Yet it wasn't.

--Think about it, my friends. Every day in the street they walk among you. They look like any of us. But they are not like us. While we quietly go about our business, they walk among us with a power, a power against which we have no defense.

There was a great tremor of fear and anticipation.

We know what that power is.

Muted murmurs of yes, yes.

It is the power to read our inmost thoughts. To sense our most private feelings. To take from us all our secrets. To take from us, ourselves.

A great sigh of affirmation passed over.

And knowing all this, what are we told? That these 'psikes' are really just like us. Just human beings who happen to have another form of perception. Per-Cep-Tion.

The last word, three separate scornful syllables drew together a hundred separate hatreds and made them one.

We are told we have protection enough. Pro-Tec-Tion. We have laws. We have the Bureau of Psyonic Management.

Jeering laughter, grown from fear and hatred.

That's our Pro-Tec-Tion from Psy Per-Cep-Tion.

Rising words drawing together, rising to unite all the disparate anxieties, uncertainties, insecurities, and all the fears they bred.

Is it?

A raging NO, a great seamless denial.

No, of course it isn't.

The leader's voice had dropped, calm now and reasonable.

As you all know, studies already indicate there are ways to control psy perception, even to block it, if necessary. We have only to look at the work of Dr. Kaslan.

Uncertainty at the name, but affirmation nonetheless.

But his research on psy suppression devices and the work of others like him, will our self-styled leaders fund it?

The briefest breathing pause.

We know the answer.

And then almost a shriek.

What is it?

No, no, rumbled in challenge and anger.

And why not? We know that too. Such research is sacrificed on the altar of appeasement. The psikes know too much and the politicians go in fear. The bribes, the scandals, the treasons. Does anyone doubt we have been traded for the politicians' security?

The rumbled response, no, no, the emotion hotter than before.

We are the ransom the powerful pay to those blackmailers. Our blood and our future is the price. Will you let yourself be sold?

No, no, the rumble rose to thunder.

While the psikes walk free, we are slaves. Our thoughts, our minds, our very being subject to them. Shall they walk free, while we go chained?

No, no, the fear and hatred ignited into flame. The conflagration roared. Engulfing. Choking.--

In it all someone was choking, literally choking on superheated air. Breath coming in gasps. Lungs heaving. Eyes blinded by acrid, choking smoke. Hold on, hold on, if you let go you'll fall into the smoke and die.

Suddenly there was a world again. The wind had dropped and the smell of approaching rain was strong. Tyler was herself. Meryl Acre had let her go.

Chapter Twenty-one

Tyler stumbled forward a few steps and felt the polished stone of the monument beneath her hands and against her face. Her breath came in convulsive gasps. Then Meryl Acre's thoughts filled her head again, only this time Tyler could distinguish her own consciousness within them.

--Bren does it rather well, don't you think? The timing, the rhythm, the rhetoric. It's all natural to him. Besides he has the one quality which brings it all together. He's a true believer. Like his followers. He knows. He has no doubts, no reservations, that you and I, and all the rest of us who are psy perceivers, are the last in a long line of last great threats to humankind. To his kind. Where is he, Tyler?--

Still struggling for breath, Tyler tried to speak. She forced out the word "No" but that was all she could manage. He's nothing, she thought, groping for some inward clarity. Somebody like Bren. Nothing. He isn't worth it. He's just another...

Meryl Acre picked up the thought and finished it for her. --He's just another lunatic in the lunatic fringe. Is that it?-- Word after word poured fluidly into Tyler's mind. --Just another street corner, beer hall genius of rabble rousing. Funny what they can do sometimes in the right time and in the right place, and riding the right wave of history. It's happened before. You get one of those impossible people who channel masses of fear and hatred. It's so irrational, you'd say, who could believe it, and you wouldn't, except it's real. And people die, sometimes not just by the thousands, but by the millions. Only of course, there aren't millions of us. That makes it a little too easy in our case. Where is he, Tyler?--

Tyler turned so her back rested against the monument. The tumult of her breathing had subsided enough for her to speak. "And you're going to save the world," she rasped. "By killing Bren, by killing those around him. Before any of this can happen." Tyler's voice was desolate, a reflection of the hopelessness she felt.

"There's a word for that, Tyler. Megalomania." This time Meryl Acre spoke aloud. She sounded almost amused. Tyler shook her head helplessly. "Is that what you think?" Meryl Acre continued speaking. "That I'm crazy enough to believe I can change the course of history by killing Martin Bren and a handful of his followers." Meryl Acre laughed softly, but bitterly. "There'll always be another Martin Bren."

"Then what are we talking about?" Tyler flung the words out. "Ten people are dead. You've killed ten people. That is insane."

"Maybe it is. But Bren and the others, they're not the ends, Tyler, they're the means." The means to what? The question rose in Tyler, but Meryl Acre answered it before it was asked. "The means of dealing with what we're facing now. It's something you know yourself. You just haven't quite figured out what it is. That little rumble, that subliminal grumbling of perception you carry around with you every time you come into metro, every time you're around conventional perceivers. You've never been able to understand it, but I can show you what it is."

As Meryl Acre spoke, Tyler could feel the persistent hum of disquiet leave its familiar place in the background of her awareness. And as it began to dominate her consciousness, it also began to assume coherence. Like a multitude of sounds slowly merging into one, innumerable bits of perception began to form into meaning.

Tyler became aware that what she perceived was the accumulation, bit by bit, of all the antagonism felt by conventional perceivers. The flick of nervousness, the ripple of apprehension, the tremor of fear, the pure clarity of hatred, disparate perceptions joined into a swell of terrifying harmony. What Tyler had heard all along were their fragmented notes. But when all the bits of perception joined, there was no mistaking the song they sang.

The accumulated response by conventional perceivers to psy perception was coalescing. The kind of coalescence which would in time, and not a long time, produce out of the common consciousness a blaze of mass hysteria. The spark which ignited it would be a great thing, or a little. It wouldn't matter. The time would find the cause. Public attitude was riding that cycle of time, a cycle which had crested and was beginning its downward journey where each forward impetus would feed the next. At the end of that journey, the accommodations and tenuous acceptance of psy perceivers lay crumbled. In their place was absolute alienation. Psy perceiver as totally other, totally monstrous. Source of fear, possible tool. Something to be controlled. Or exploited. Or killed.

Tyler would have said such knowledge was impossible. She would have said that, but could no longer. Forced to it, she recognized at last the source of that whine of perception which had bedeviled her for so long. Reluctantly she bowed her understanding and assented, acknowledging the truth of what she was experiencing. With her acquiescence, the upswell of perception broke, and dwindled once again into the background of her awareness. Then Meryl Acre's words filled her mind again.

--It is happening, you know. How old are you, Tyler? Twenty-eight? No, twenty-nine. We won't make it through your life and mine. Within a generation, conventionals will not tolerate us free among them.

--If we were just another category of alienness, like all the others people have used before, something to be objectified into something less than human, we might, at least, be allowed to survive. But that won't work this time.

--When human beings turn on themselves, creating out of each other the thing to be feared, to be used, to be destroyed, they indulge themselves in the ever satisfying belief in the other's inferiority. Moral, physical, mental, whatever. That conviction justifies how they savage each other. But it also, eventually, puts some limit on what they do. Because no matter how great the fear, the revulsion, the contempt of one human being for another, they keep the solacing balm that they are superior to what they fear and despise.

--But that won't work with us because we really are what all that self-hatred and self-doubt has feared through human history. We really are superior. We really do have a special capability. It gives us a distinctive source of knowledge, therefore what they consider a distinctive source of power. And they will not let us live with that.--

Suddenly the relentless, invasive words ceased. In their place, a silence like something from the beginning of time. And then a voice. "Tyler."

Tyler found herself clinging to the monument, half sitting, half lying, against it. She was hugging it so tightly that her arm was locked in cramp. Her breath rose and fell heavily. She hung there for a moment feeling the smooth, cool surface of the stone as if to rediscover reality there.

Slowly she raised her head. Meryl Acre stood without moving, watching her. Tyler could sort nothing in Meryl Acre except a strange amalgam of pity and detachment. Laboriously Tyler pushed herself upright, but her legs would not support her. She leaned heavily against the monument. Meryl Acre stirred, as if to come to her aid, but she stopped. She paused as if considering what to do. Finally she said, "That's the knowledge I have to contend with. And now so do you."

"No," Tyler said and then with great effort, --NO.-- But Tyler's denials, spoken and imparted, scattered like leaves in the wind before the irresistible clarity of her own perception, her long awaited comprehension of that buzzing disquiet which had been growing in her through the years. In desperation she seized the one piece of logic that managed to surface in her consciousness. "Even if it were true, this vision you've led me to, is this your answer? To become the very thing their fears create?"

"*If* it is true, Tyler?" Meryl Acre's voice was heavy with scorn. "You know it is. You know it's not something I've imagined or invented. So what was I supposed to do? Call a press conference? Maybe have Laurence give a speech?"

Through her weakness and rising despair, Tyler's anger flashed. "What am I, Alice to your Queen of Hearts? Off with their heads. Kill everyone who hates psy perceivers. Declare war on the rest of the humanity for what they might do tomorrow? It's madness. You know it is."

"Part of what's bothering you, Tyler, is you don't sense any madness in me."

"Maybe not. But it's there, Meryl. It's there."

"Are you so sure?"

"Yes. Only madness would bring to life the very thing that drives the fear. Would become the monster that only lives, should only live, in the fantasies of a man like Bren and people like him. And in so doing, fulfills the prophecy that only lives in your own mind."

"And now in yours, Tyler. Don't forget that."

Tyler finally took a step forward, her hand resting on the monument to steady herself. The first drops of rain were beginning to fall. "Come with me. Turn yourself in. Put an end to this, before it's too late."

"I will put an end to it. Before it's too late. And that means I need this one more, this last one. I need Bren. I need him to tilt the probability into the certainty range. Because you still don't quite understand. All of this has been to bring about exactly what you and Jonas are trying to prevent. I've intended all along for these deaths to become public. Who do you think put Toller onto things?

"You see, if we wait for time to unfold at its leisure, it'll be too late. Slowly, inevitably, we'll conform to what society asks of us. We're too empathetic not too. And then someday we'll look back and wonder how we came to be where we'll end up. If any of us survive, that is.

"Bren and his chosen few, they gave me a target I could justify. No matter what you want to think, I couldn't kill at random. And the people I killed, they really are, were, dangerous, terribly dangerous. Led by Bren, tapping into that wellspring of hatred you feel every day, they could have unleashed a flood which could have drowned us, not in thirty or forty years, but far more quickly." A shadow passed over Meryl Acre's face. Then collecting herself, she said, "But stopping Bren, that won't accomplish anything permanent. Who knows when the next imp of history will come along. As it surely will.

"We psy perceivers need to understand. Now. We need to know what's happening to us. We need to know, now, that our place in human history is dissolving, running away like sand beneath our feet. The fears, the jealousies, the hatreds of the non-psy are too great. And so we can see, before it's too late, I'm forcing the crisis. Forcing it to break upon us while we can still do something about it.

"When this series of murders blazes through the public awareness, there'll be no going back to the status quo. The hatred which is building through time will be revealed. And we will understand we can no longer be compliant, anxious to please, hoping to win acceptance by cooperation. We'll no longer be able pretend we're going to be allowed to fit in the world of those who consider themselves 'normal.' Because they will no longer let us.

"You and I, Tyler, have been blessed, or cursed, with extraordinary knowledge. We both have a sense of what is inevitable. What I've done will provoke the reaction which will bring that knowledge to the rest of us. It will draw the lines between us and them soon enough for it to matter."

Meryl Acre's calm certainty seemed impenetrable. In desperation, Tyler cried out, "And Jonas, is he one of *them*?"

Meryl's expression did not change, but inwardly she smiled. "Jonas. That is a touch, I do confess." She was quiet for a moment. "I love him. My love for him aside, he's a good man. But yes, in the final analysis, Jonas is one of them. He'll have no choice. He, people like him, they'll be overwhelmed by the rest. Eventually people like Jonas, they'll either accept the reality the rest of the world creates or privately nurture their own doubts and disquiets. They might help, here and there, as 'good' people always have. But they won't be able to protect us. Our survival can't depend on the Jonases of the world, but on ourselves.

"And that's why I'm going to finish what I started. I'm going to kill Martin Bren, like I killed the others. I'm going to ensure that Wilkins has to bring this out, has to make it public. After that, I don't much care what happens to me. But for now, I can't let you stop me. I've come too far to fail now. Tell me where Martin Bren's going to be tonight, Tyler."

Tyler resisted. She tried to return her own insistent conviction that Meryl Acre was caught in an insane confusion between belief and knowledge. She tried to force a clear thought, to plead for Meryl Acre to surrender, to accept that it was all madness. But Meryl Acre took Tyler's thought and made it echo, mockingly, through her mind.

--Maybe you're right. Maybe I am crazy. Maybe Martin Bren is just a figment of my demented imagination. And the persistent unrest you feel, maybe that, too, is just your imagination. Try to believe that, console yourself with that, Tyler, that all of this is just a construct of my insanity. But, in the meantime, tell me, where is Martin Bren, Tyler, where is Martin Bren?--

Nothing existed but the hammering question.

--Wherewherewhere is Martin Bren?--

In a state beyond thought, even beyond emotion, Tyler's screening broke and Meryl Acre learned what she wanted to know. With the knowledge, sorrow and regret returned.

--Only none of it is my madness. It's theirs. And it will kill us. Or enslave us. And I will not let that happen, not easily. I will not let you stop me, Tyler. I cannot let you stop me. I hope you know how deep is my regret.--

The regret deepened into aching sorrow. A sorrow, no longer prophetic, but totally present. Then the sorrow itself gave way. In its place the familiar unsettled dis-ease drifted back. It came first like scattered flakes, and then thicker they fell, until they became a storm of dark snow, sharp and crystalline. The black snow fell thicker and thicker until its accumulating crystals had blotted out all light, all air. Then sight and breath were gone, shut away in a world that had gone to glass, smooth, impervious, and blacker than the void before time began.

Death could have come quietly then but the glass shattered, raining inward, an onslaught of stinging shards. Fried psy fried psy fried psy. Hate them hate them hate them. Harder and faster they fell. Friedpsy friedpsy friedpsy. Hatethem hatethem hatethem. A storm as of a million on a million tiny edges which shredded first skin, then muscle, then bone until all that was left was the consciousness which bore the pain and despaired at its own destruction. Only somewhere, faint but persistent, sorrow and regret. Hopelessly, desperately, the dissolving consciousness which had been Tyler West cried out to that sorrow and regret. Help me. Meryl, help me. Dying it cried out, help me.

And then only dissolution.

The rain was falling now. Tyler lay at the base of the monument. Her face was pressed down. Her hands, contorted and stiff, clutched at the sodden ground. It looked as if a great force had tried to push her through the earth. Meryl Acre stood above her. The rain fell on them both, not fiercely, but steadily, relentlessly.

Meryl Acre went to her knees beside Tyler and turned her over. Tyler's face was rigid. The rain washed away the dirt from her nose and mouth, but it did not wash away the lines of agony into which her face was set.

Meryl Acre watched the labored rise and fall of Tyler's ribs as she struggled for breath, the clenching and unclenching in her throat as she tried to swallow air.

Meryl Acre dragged Tyler up until her back was propped against the base of the monument, the rain no longer running in her nose and mouth. Meryl Acre got up. For a long moment she stood looking down at Tyler. "I need to kill you, Tyler. I need to kill you. But I can't." Then she turned and walked away.

Chapter Twenty-two

Dorian resisted the insistent sound as long as she could. Although still more asleep than awake, she knew the sound shouldn't be there. It was her phone and she had set it for message only. That realization brought her fully awake. The call was from someone who had authorization to override the block she had put on it. Most likely then the police. Or maybe Jonas. She glanced at the time and said "Shit" under her breath.

She selected audio out, video and audio in, and let her voice deliberately go sharp with irritation. "Dorian Rath, here. It's late."

The answering voice was abrupt and unidentifiable. The incoming video was scrambled, its image reduced to noise.

"Tyler West needs help. Riscoll Monument, the park across from her hotel."

"What the hell...who is this?"

"Tell Tyler, I couldn't do it." The voice paused briefly. "Not to one of us. But I will finish it tonight. No matter what." Dorian thought she heard desperation in those words, but a strange sense of calm or even relief as well. Before she could respond, the caller had broken off.

Staring at the now blank display, Dorian listened to the silence of the disengaged signal. Her first thought was to try to contact Tyler. She reached for her phone, but stopped. Go now. She didn't wait to consider further. Go now. Impelled by the inner command, she called down for her ceevee. Then dressed quickly and left. Tyler's hotel and the park were only a few blocks away.

— Dorian's hurried drive through the rain slicked streets and into the sodden park might have been born of a hunch, but the hunch felt more like the certainty of knowledge. So much so, that when she found Tyler, there was no surprise in it. She knelt beside her. The rain had stopped but Tyler was drenched, her coat soaked through and muddy. Dorian took her by the shoulders and, supporting her, pulled her away from the cold stone of the monument. She felt a slight tremor go through the muscles of Tyler's back and shoulders.

"Tyler," Dorian said gently. She got no response. All she could sort in Tyler was a strange morass of disorientation, a mental state at some indefinable point between awareness and unconsciousness. She tried impartment. --Tyler.-- But she got back a wave of revulsion so strong she broke off abruptly. She reached up and put her hand on Tyler's face. Tyler's head weaved slightly. Then Dorian sorted a flash of panic which quickly subsided into confusion. Tyler opened her eyes but they didn't seem focused on anything.

"Tyler. It's Dorian. Tyler."

Slowly Tyler raised her arm. She grasped Dorian as if reassuring herself that Dorian was real.

"Can you stand?" Dorian asked.

They staggered to their feet, Dorian using the monument to support them. For a moment, she thought Tyler's knees would buckle, but Tyler threw her weight back against the monument and managed to stay upright. For a while, she just leaned there, her breath coming in long deep gasps. Then she began to shiver.

"Here." Dorian helped Tyler out of her soggy coat, then took off her own coat and awkwardly draped it over Tyler's shoulders. "I'll get some help," Dorian said.

Tyler's hand tightened its grip on Dorian's arm. "Just...wait a minute." She took a few ragged breaths. "I'll be all right, I think." Her voice rasped with effort.

Dorian tried to sort what she could from Tyler, but out of the traumatized chaos which was Tyler's constant, she could extract only one meaningful thing. Tyler had felt herself dying and now had to adapt to being alive.

In an outburst of frustration, Dorian shouted to the night air, "Get over here and help us. I know you're out there somewhere." But running feet sounded on the path even before she had finished. Then she and Tyler were caught in a glare of white light. From the darkness behind the glare came doubt and apprehension. Tyler wavered and Dorian grabbed for her, feeling the drag of her weight. "Help us." Dorian spit out the words.

Decisiveness replaced doubt, if not apprehension, and a stocky man came forward from behind the light. "I'm Torres. Enforcement," he said. Behind him, another man was dimly visible.

With a mixture of relief and resentment, Dorian looked at them. "My shadows," she said. "Good for something. At last."

Torres walked up quickly and joined her. Between them they held Tyler. She continued to shiver uncontrollably and would have fallen without their support. Tyler's awareness had subsided into a state of numbed shock, through which a name occasionally floated, a name so unlikely Dorian could not quite accept its significance.

"Let's try to get her back to the hotel," Dorian said. Torres gestured uncertainly, doubt reasserting itself within him, but Dorian ignored it. To Tyler she said, "Come on. Try to walk."

With their aid, Tyler took a couple of stumbling steps forward. At a word from Torres, his partner swung the light away from them to illumine the walkway. They began to make their way in a straggled procession, Dorian and Torres with Tyler between them, his partner following behind.

When they reached the end of the walkway across from the hotel, Tyler mumbled, "Not the hotel. Get a car." She spoke with difficulty as if her throat could not open to let the words out.

"Tyler, you can't..." Dorian began.

Frustrated urgency flooded through Tyler. Get a car, she thought fiercely. Just get us to a car.

"Get your ceevee." Dorian said to Torres. She could feel him resist an order from her. She nodded at Tyler. "You know she's been working with Chief Wilkins and Commissioner Acre." He inclined his head noncommittally. "She wants a car."

Torres ran through a series of rapid calculations, not the least of which was that, whatever status T. West had, it was unofficial. Balanced against that had been a secret briefing from the Chief that West and Commissioner Acre were lending the department some discreet assistance and should be given every possible consideration. And that, in Torres' mind, added up to something as troubling as it was important. Something his surveillance assignment on D. Rath was part of. Something about which his own knowledge was incomplete, which in turn meant that any decisions were hazardous. He thought about all these things, then he told his partner, "Bring the car over."

His partner ran to their ceevee, jumped in, and pulled up along side of them. They put Tyler in the back seat and Dorian climbed in next to her. Torres got in front.

"Where?" Torres asked.

"Tyler?" Dorian encouraged.

Third and Birch, Tyler thought groggily.

Dorian repeated the street names out loud and then sorted recognition from Torres even before he spoke. "That area's tagged." he said. "Important stakeout. Trying to locate a material witness." Dorian wasn't sure, but it seemed like he believed his version. She wondered just how much Chief Wilkins had told his own men. She also wondered how much of her own guess work was true. Particularly she wondered about Meryl Acre. That was the unlikely name playing in Tyler's head.

She looked at Tyler who slouched limply beside her. Tyler's shivering had subsided, but her face was etched with strain. Her eyes were open but they seemed to be staring blankly at some inner vision.

Dorian leaned over Torres' shoulder. "Just get us there. Quietly if you have to, but get us there. And give me that coffee." She pointed to the cup that sat in the console next to Torres. He handed the cup back. Dorian held it and Tyler sipped from it.

Torres glanced back at them, assessed Tyler and then said to his partner. "Third and Birch. Fast. And careful."

As they drove, Torres placed a call. He entered a code which produced a series of re-direct beeps. Finally he got an answer. He identified himself and gave their location. Then he said, "Can I get through to the Chief?"

There was another series of beeps and then sharply a voice said, "Wilkins."

Torres, catching the tone, didn't bother with preliminaries. "Chief, I'm on my way to the stakeout on Birch Street. I've got Rath and West with me."

Without hesitating, Wilkins cut in. "Let me talk to Tyler."

Torres said, "I don't think she can."

Dorian reached over and took the phone, handing back the coffee as she did. "This is Dorian Rath. I'm not sure what's happened, but I've got a pretty good idea. Tyler's pretty foggy. All I know is, you better watch out for Meryl Acre."

"Meryl Acre," the Chief repeated, his voice rising in surprise.

An inrush of breath sounded from the phone, but it didn't come from Chief Wilkins. Then Jonas' voice spoke in a tight whisper which wanted to be a shout, "Meryl. What in the hell's Meryl got to do with this?"

Dorian felt Tyler stir beside her. "I'm not sure," Dorian said quietly. "But whatever happened to Tyler tonight. Your wife is part of it."

Dorian imagined she could feel the heaviness of Jonas' silence. Then Wilkins' voice came through again. "Tyler OK?"

"I'm not sure. I think so. She was able to give me the address. Should we keep coming?"

"Yeah."

Dorian gave the phone back to Torres who nodded while Wilkins gave instructions.

Without the siren on, it took them about ten minutes to drive east and south from the elegant neighborhood of Tyler's hotel to the general vicinity of 3rd and Birch. In that time, Tyler slowly returned to herself, a process Dorian observed with a fascination she could not suppress. At the end of it, more quickly than Dorian would have thought possible, Tyler had re-established an almost normal constant, badly shaken, but definitely controlled, and once again carefully screened.

"You called the Chief." Tyler's voice was low but steady at last.

"Yeah."

"What did you tell him?"

"I couldn't tell him much. I don't know much." Dorian felt a flick of response from Tyler. "I told him to watch out for Meryl Acre." Dorian accompanied her words with a strong sense of query.

But Tyler, leaning forward, turned her attention to Torres. "They don't have Bren yet." It wasn't really a question.

"They're still out there. I assume not," Torres said.

Even with Tyler's careful screening, the tightness of worry was evident in her. More questions rose in Dorian, but Tyler, with a slight twist of her head, gave an almost imperceptible gesture of dismissal. Then she leaned back against the seat cushions and they rode on in silence.

Chapter Twenty-three

The 300 block of Birch Street was a weary stretch of ground floor storefronts, many abandoned, and mostly boarded up second floors. From corner to corner, orange light contended with the darkness.

Martin Bren shuffled past the front of the building he had used in the past without looking at it. As he made his way, he stopped occasionally to rummage in overflowing trash containers which seemed rarely to have been emptied. To anyone watching, he would appear to be just a bit of human debris himself. But everything was quiet. There was no reason for it to be otherwise. No one knew about him, not the police and, as for the bureaucrats, he lived his life keeping himself hidden from them. But he had greater enemies than those. Crayton, Randle, the rest, they hadn't been accidents, he was sure of that. Whoever had killed them wanted him dead too.

From the shadow of a doorway a few yards away, Bren peered back in the direction he had come. Then he began his shuffling progress again. But when he came to the corner of 3rd street, he turned, went the half block to a narrow alley and started back along it. The alley was dark. Almost no light from the street lamps reached it. The darkness felt like safety, but Martin Bren knew that was deceptive. If the police, or worse, if the psikes were watching for him, the darkness would not hide him. A few doors away, he could dimly make out the small overhang of roof which covered the back door he was heading for. He'd have to decide soon. He fumbled in his pocket for the key, and let his fingers close over it. His breath came more quickly. The risk needed to be taken.

But a few steps short of the doorway, he heard, "Free thought forever." The whisper of words came from the darkness and Martin Bren's heart thudded wildly. Before he could react further, the whisper continued. "Don't look around. Don't stop. They're watching."

"Who are you?" Martin Bren's words were almost inaudible.

"A friend. Free thought forever."

Martin Bren let go of the key and kept walking.

Chapter Twenty-four

For Isa Wilkins, it had been a long, uncertain, and unprofitable night. The tip which Tyler West had relayed about Martin Bren's whereabouts seemed unlikely to pay off but he could not ignore it. Still he couldn't help wondering whether it was an elaborate diversion which Laurence Meredith had devised for his own purposes. He wondered if Tyler had thought about that too.

And he would have been a lot happier if Jonas had stayed away, but Jonas had insisted on coming along, and Wilkins had decided he couldn't deny him. Jonas had more faith in Meredith than he did. Jonas had managed to convince himself that getting Bren would actually accomplish something. To Chief Wilkins, at best it only promised an indefinite loose end.

And now the call from Torres, which had left him and Jonas stunned but for different reasons.

At first, Jonas was so angry he couldn't speak. Then, thrusting the phone he had seized from him back at Wilkins, he said, "Damn Dorian. God damn her." The words weren't idle expletives. They were a real curse.

"Jonas, calm down," Wilkins said.

"Dorian and her goddamn need to call attention to herself." Jonas' voice was shaking.

Jonas' anger was so palpable the Chief wondered how it would have struck Dorian herself, or even Tyler. Not for the first time in his life, Chief Wilkins was glad he was not a psy perceiver. He had enough to do to handle Jonas' anger from observation without having

173

to feel it, too. And Jonas' anger was only part of his concern. He had to deal with the rest of the implications of that call. The presence of Dorian Rath for starters. And what in the hell was wrong with Tyler? Wilkins glanced unobtrusively at Jonas, still obviously fuming beside him. He felt a hollow certainty that Jonas was wrong. The mention of Meryl Acre's name was not Dorian Rath's attempt at grandstanding. But Meryl Acre. That was beyond belief. What he needed, Wilkins thought urgently, was to talk to Tyler.

Restlessly, Wilkins checked the time. They'd arrive soon, even with Torres being cautious about how he came to the stakeout.

The voice of one of his surveillance team sounded. "Chief, that wino who went by a few minutes ago. He's in the alley now, heading back west."

"Anything else?"

"Another pross. This one's on 3rd, going north, probably on her way to the District."

"Where is she now?"

"Should be just crossing the alley on 3rd between Birch and Newbridge." A brief pause. "Chief, no location. I've lost her."

Isa Wilkins felt a sharp leap of intuition. "Where's the wino?" he demanded.

"Just about to exit the alley at 4th. Seems OK."

But everything in Isa Wilkins denied it. Without hesitation, he snapped out his commands. "Lights now. Helos in. Lights. Full perimeter."

Almost instantly, spotlights hit the alley and the neighboring streets. Their white glare washed out the orange glow of the street lamps and made sharp patterns of black shadow. A distant drone got rapidly louder and, in moments, helos added a further bath of white light from above. Spotted in the middle of the unremitting glare was the seemingly insignificant figure of the wino who cowered once, then began to run back into the alley.

But he was surrounded by voices which called out, "Stop. Police. Martin Bren. Stop."

Rising over the others, an amplified voice rang out. "Martin Bren. This is Wilkins, Chief of Police. We believe your life is in danger. Stay where you are. It's urgent you stay where you are. Let us come to you. We're here to protect you."

The circle of voices had closed upon Bren and he wavered. Then he burst forward, ran hard into the nearest enforcement officer, knocked him down, almost lost his own footing, but recovered and in the unrelenting light ran desperately back down the alley toward 3rd.

At the back door he had passed before, he stopped. With shaking hands, he raised the key to the door. They hadn't chased him. They hadn't chased him because they knew they had him, but he had to hide, try to hide. Men at the other end of the alley, at 3rd Street, stood waiting.

--Free thought forever.--

In the moment of his despair, the slogan rang in Bren's head. It promised victory, complete and irrevocable victory.

--Free thought forever.--

Martin Bren's hand fell away from the door. There was an instant in which he was aware of the impossible incongruity between the panic he'd been feeling and the triumphant words which had suddenly filled his head.

To those watching, to Isa Wilkins hurrying forward, trailed by Jonas Acre. To the officers poised for further instructions from Wilkins. To Torres and his partner spilling out of the car which had just pulled into the alley at its intersection with 3rd Street. To Tyler and Dorian who followed more slowly. To all of them, it appeared that Bren had at last realized the futility of his position. He turned from the door. He dropped the key, but didn't seem to notice.

"Wait there. Let me come to you," Chief Wilkins called out.

In the cold white light, the play of expression on Bren's face was clearly visible. As he turned, he looked like an actor about to begin a dramatic scene. But in an instant he became a puppet. His arms and legs jerked in rigid movement. He stumbled forward.

And in that instant, Tyler and Dorian perceived what the rest had not yet seen. Shadowed in a recessed angle where the back of one building jutted out farther than the rest was another presence.

"No." Tyler's voice rose, hoarse with desperation. Bren's movements had become a convulsive dance. Two of the officers had darted forward to grab him, but his arms shot out with such force that the men were knocked off balance. Tyler shouted again. "No, Meryl, no." Instinctively Tyler extended her arm. A spotlight followed the direction she pointed. Caught now in the light and clearly visible to the Chief and to Jonas was the other person, a woman, garishly dressed, even more garishly painted.

With a shudder of recognition but without comprehension, Jonas Acre breathed his wife's name. "Meryl?"

Bren stumbled forward, almost colliding again with the two officers who had run up to him. His head came up. His face burned with the hatred that was consuming him.

Chief Wilkins had drawn a gun, a lethal weapon, not a hazer. He looked past Bren and stared at the streetwalker. Only with difficulty could he recognize behind her makeup the person of Jonas' wife. He looked to Tyler, asking without words for the last help she could give him. In answer, she filled his mind with anguished confirmation.

--It is Meryl Acre. It's been Meryl Acre all along. She's killing him. Now.--

Isa Wilkins fired, three rounds rapidly. Meryl Acre flew backward into the angle of the building, hung upright for a moment, and then slid, crumpled, at its base.

"Meryl." No whisper this time from Jonas but a high unnatural shriek voicing a pain that would never be appeased. Not in Jonas who felt it nor in Tyler who, despairing, shared it with him.

Chief Wilkins and his men rushed forward to Martin Bren, but his face had already flared into blankness and he, like Meryl Acre, had fallen into final silence.

Chapter Twenty-five

The off-road ceevee swung smoothly along the graveled drive and stopped in front of the old stone house. Dorian Rath got out. She waited for a moment, her sharp green eyes assessing her surroundings. The house stood before her, calm and silent, secure in the protection of the trees which sheltered it. It occurred to Dorian she didn't know what kind of trees they were. Their leaves were still summer bright, but the fresh coolness of the afternoon already promised the frost which would soon turn them from green to bronze and finally to dull, dead brown. Dorian tried to picture the scene before her smothered in snow. The thought made her shiver slightly.

Except for the ceaseless rustle of the leaves, everything seemed quiet, deserted. Yet she knew she was expected and that Tyler was not far away. She followed a flagstone walk around the corner of the house. It led to a small patio set out with an appropriately rustic table and chairs. The house itself was L-shaped and the patio fit in the angle. The longer portion of the L had obviously been added at one time to the shorter end which formed the front of the house. Still even that more recent part of the house was old, and all of stone and wood.

Dorian was about to return to the front when a head appeared in a door set in the long side of the house. A woman came out, wiping her hands on a cloth. She was a little more than middle-aged but not quite elderly.

"D. Rath?" she asked politely. Dorian nodded. "I'm sorry I didn't hear you arrive. I've been trying to finish up a little cleaning. Tyler is out riding. She'll be back anytime."

Dorian nodded again and they both stood awkwardly. Dorian sorted a couple of things immediately. The woman, obviously Tyler's housekeeper, was curious about her and a little skittish. Not apprehensive. Just skittish. Also she wasn't at all worried that Tyler was slightly overdue from her ride.

"I'm sure Tyler mentioned your name, but I don't recall it," Dorian said. Dorian sorted the name before it was spoken, but she waited for the answer.

The woman flashed a quick embarrassed smile. "I don't know where my head is today. R. Fuentes. Rita." She gave one last swipe of the cloth across her hands and then stuck one out. "Pleased to meet you." Dorian took the offered hand. Rita Fuentes gestured toward the door. "Won't you come in."

"I'm perfectly content to sit out here." Dorian pointed toward the table and chairs. "Out of your way. I don't need to be entertained."

The housekeeper looked a little doubtful, but Dorian sorted that she was grateful as well. Her mind was on the work she wanted to finish. And the skittishness she felt, Dorian realized, was not so much over Dorian herself but over the simple fact of her visit. R. Fuentes guarded Tyler's privacy more out of loyalty than duty.

"If you're sure. But you will let me bring you something. Tea. Coffee. Perhaps a glass of wine."

"Thanks. I'd like some coffee. Black."

Rita Fuentes stepped back into the house but returned shortly carrying a tray that held an insulated pitcher and two mugs. The coffee was excellent and from the speed with which it arrived, Dorian was sure that rustic though the setting might be, the kitchen was current. No boiling water over a gas jet or electric coil.

Rita Fuentes hesitated slightly. "Is there anything else I can get you?"

"This is fine," Dorian replied.

"Tyler will be here soon. She...ah...tends to lose track of time when she's riding." Especially lately, Rita Fuentes might have added, but didn't.

The housekeeper re-entered the house and Dorian sat, drinking her coffee and thinking. Mostly about why she had felt so strong a need to make this visit. The project for IsogaCorp had kept her away almost two months, but she'd come back east as soon as she was free. To see Tyler. She hadn't even considered asking Tyler to come into metro. Dorian had come to her.

Dorian looked around her again. She tried to remember the last time she had been in an environment quite so countrified, but she couldn't. Maybe she never had. It was unquestionably beautiful here, but she could not imagine herself spending very much time in this splendid isolation. An afternoon yes, a couple of days, a week, maybe. Living here? Impossible. But not for Tyler.

As far as Dorian knew, Tyler hadn't been back into metro since the deaths of Meryl Acre and Martin Bren. There had been no need. Jonas and Isa Wilkins had done their work well. The only publicity in the aftermath of that night in the alley had focused on illegal activities by Laurence and the League for Psy Rights. Hardin Toller, the broadcast media, the blogs had had a field day with that. The death of Martin Bren had been shunted into insignificance, unable to compete for interest with the scandal over the League. As for Meryl Acre, the media had been hungry for that story, too. But the story they got was that the wife of Jonas Acre, Commissioner for the Bureau of Psyonic Management, had long had serious involvement with major anti-psy groups. Conflicts over her husband's job had led to unmanageable pressures, growing instability, and ultimately, suicide. The media and the blogs loved it. It provided just the right kind of titillating personal material to give an interesting slant to even the most pedestrian reporting and commentary. All of it, information on the League, Bren, Meryl Acre, had been carefully spun, but Dorian doubted even Tyler knew all the details of how that had been accomplished. But however it had been done, the real story, the murders Meryl Acre had committed, had been silenced. In that much at least, Jonas and Wilkins, and, yes, even Tyler, had been successful.

When Tyler finally arrived she didn't come through the house. She came striding toward Dorian along a path that led from the back of the property. She didn't dawdle but she didn't seem to be in a particular rush either. She was dressed for riding in a shirt, breeches, and well-worn but very well-fitting boots. The breeches were of modern cut and obviously made of some high tech stretch fabric but the boots were certainly made of genuine leather.

Tyler walked up, bringing with her the scent of horse. She had been carrying a riding helmet which she set on the table. All normal social screening was in place. "Sorry to keep you waiting," she said. "I'll go in, clean up and change."

"Don't bother on my account." Dorian looked at Tyler and let her amusement surface. "You do add to the picturesque."

Without sitting, Tyler poured herself a mug of coffee. "Too bad we don't get more traffic through here," she said tartly. "I could hang out a sign for tourists."

It seemed almost inevitable for them to fall into the old sniping kind of exchange. It wasn't exactly the tone Dorian wanted but it seemed the only one available. She couldn't tell whether Tyler was sharing the joke or whether she was offended.

"I just meant..." Dorian began. She broke off. "You look tired. Why don't you sit and have your coffee." Dorian made no attempt to screen the fact she found the setting eccentric but it was also clear she trying not to aggravate.

Tyler looked at her for a moment and then sat. "I rode harder than I'd planned," she said. "That's why I'm late. It took a little longer to cool down."

"I guess that means the horse."

Tyler's head came up. "Yes, the horse," she said dryly.

"It's OK. I didn't mind waiting." Tyler continued to drink her coffee, her expression watchful, her screening secure. Observing her, Dorian said, "I think of that as your clickety-click expression."

"What does that mean?"

"It means the analytic machinery is going full bore and you're trying to figure out why I'm here. But I'm not sure I'm worth the effort in this case. I don't think my motives are really very complicated. I guess I just wanted to see how you are."

"That seems a bit sentimental. For you."

Dorian sighed and lowered her head. Tyler could no longer see her face, only that cap of startling white blonde hair. After a moment Dorian raised her head and said, "You're just a little more acute than I am. It bugs me."

It was Tyler's turn to look away. "Psy perception isn't a talent, it's just another physical sense." She looked back at Dorian. "Maybe one in which too much acuity isn't particularly desirable." And then the level of Tyler's screening changed. Suddenly Dorian could tell Tyler was thinking not only of herself, but of Meryl Acre as well.

Dorian answered the thought. "She really was crazy, you know." Dorian spoke very quietly, but her eyes glittered.

"That would seem to be the most sensible opinion." Tyler's voice was hard edged.

Dorian pushed her coffee aside and leaned over the table. The urgency in her was out of character. "Surely, you don't have any doubts about that." But even as she spoke, she knew she was wrong. Meryl Acre and her sanity, or lack of it, was a source of tormenting ambivalence for Tyler. "She killed eleven people. She almost killed you." Frustration made Dorian's voice high and sharp.

"Almost," Tyler said flatly. Beyond that, she remained expressionless.

Her unresponsiveness provoked Dorian. "Damn it, Tyler, not killing you is hardly proof of Meryl Acre's sanity."

Dorian immediately regretted her outburst. It seemed she and Tyler couldn't avoid sparring matches. But to her surprise, a wave of amusement passed through Tyler. "Seemed like pretty good evidence to me." The inner laughter passed quickly, however, like a brief gleam of sunshine through overpowering clouds. "But personal bias aside, I'll tell you, I don't believe she was insane. If by that you mean, acting irrationally."

Impatience fluttered through Dorian. "There must be some reason it's so important for you to deny the obvious." Tyler ignored the opening. Dorian didn't press the point. She took a sip of coffee, then let her gaze wander to the fields behind the house. Still looking away, she asked, "How's Jonas?"

She could feel Tyler give a slight shrug. "Still on leave. Cal's filling in."

Dorian looked back. Tyler's expression remained as neutral as the tone of her words. "He'll get over it," Dorian said. Tyler shrugged again, a gesture neither of assent nor denial. Dorian thought for a moment, then added. "I never liked Jonas all that much. Combination of conscientious bureaucrat and master manipulator." Tyler didn't budge. Dorian felt a rising anger, but tamped it down. "And he is the one who pulled you into this mess in the first place."

"Is the corollary to that, he deserves what he got?"

"A response. At last."

"Jonas," Tyler said wearily. "He always did as well as he could. For someone who had more than one master to serve." She paused. "And he did...does...care about us. Psy perceivers."

"He will come back from this, Tyler,"

"I hope you're right." Lingering after the words was Tyler's awareness that whatever Jonas recovered, he would never recover any real friendship with her. Tyler pushed the regret of that away. "Since you seem so interested in mopping up, I assume you've heard about the League."

"Yeah," Dorian said glumly.

"Wilkins always said he might have to throw Toller a bone."

"And Laurence is it."

"Toller will see the League completely dismantled before he finishes."

"Laurence knew what he was doing."

Tyler nodded and let a little of her own anger surface. "Jonas, Wilkins. They needed Laurence's information all along. With it, they could have stopped this thing a lot sooner. They could have had what they needed if the League hadn't been forced to operate illegally."

"Do I detect some latent activism? Laurence would think *that* was something, at least." Dorian smiled unpleasantly. "But I'll tell you, Tyler, it'll be cold day in hell before it's legal for you or me, or any psy, to wander around unidentified. Even the people who hire me, they want what I can give them, but they sure don't want it turned on them. They don't mind using us. Like Jonas used you. But they're never going to trust us. Not really. All we can do is carve out the best niche we can. And to that end, whatever you feel about the outcome of all this, and its effects on Jonas or Laurence or even you, you know that reporting about 'illegal surveillance by League for Psy Rights' beats the hell out of 'psyonic murder spree.' You may think it's a bad end, but it's not as bad as it could be."

"That's quite a speech for you, Dorian."

Dorian caught the sarcasm in Tyler. "Patronize me if you want, but you know I'm right."

"Do I?" Tyler's voice was a harsh whisper, her words all but drowned in a torrent of doubt and despair. Driven by the force of her own emotions, Tyler stood up and turned away so suddenly that her chair rattled clumsily behind her. She walked a few steps away and stood with her back to Dorian.

Whether intentionally or not, the flood of Tyler's emotions had swept over Dorian unscreened. Shaken by that intensity, Dorian sat silently for a moment, then got up and stood behind Tyler. "Oh, Tyler, Meryl Acre didn't kill you, but she sure left her mark." The sympathy in her was true and unalloyed.

Tyler sorted the sympathy and found herself, not resenting it, but taking consolation from it. They stood in silence until Tyler abruptly said, "Let's walk." Without waiting, she turned and started along the path that led back away from the house. Tyler didn't appear to be hurrying, but by the time Dorian followed her, she found herself having to trot to catch up.

Chapter Twenty-six

Tyler and Dorian walked the length of the house and continued on. A little distance behind the house and off to the left was a building even Dorian recognized as a stable. Tyler led the way until they came to a fence. The fence was post and rail, made of actual wood as far a Dorian could tell, and well weathered. Running lengthwise back to the stable, it formed the near side of what was obviously a horse paddock, now empty. Beyond its farther side, cleared fields gave way to woods.

Tyler leaned her arms on the top rail and looked off toward the woods. Dorian joined her and waited. After a while, Tyler said, "I'm trying to decide whether you're the least likely confidant. Or the inevitable one." Behind Tyler's words was a mockery that encompassed both of them. It made Dorian smile and Tyler knew it although they didn't look at each other. "Tell me," Tyler asked, "what do you think was more insane, what Meryl Acre did or her motive for doing it?"

The question disconcerted Dorian. "I never thought of separating the two. They're both crazy. Utterly crazy." Dorian thought for a minute. "But if you pressed me for a distinction, then the motive is the real craziness."

"Yes, I once said to Jonas, the problem with this business was hypothesizing a method only a psy could use for acts which would inevitably lead to a result no psy would want."

"That's right, and that's what establishes Meryl Acre's insanity," Dorian insisted, as if it were vital to her that Tyler concede the point.

"Her insanity. Killing people, deliberately to inflame the passions of the non-psy population. Nothing could be crazier than that."

"I told you before. I know that's not true. Or at least, I know it's an oversimplification." Tyler turned to look at Dorian. "You see, Meryl Acre had a reason, a substantial reason, to believe her actions were, not only worth the risk, but a way to prevent something even more catastrophic." Dorian allowed her skepticism to surface, clear and undiluted. Tyler noted the reaction, but continued, "She had an awareness, a knowledge, she couldn't ignore. She was able to perceive that accumulating among conventional perceivers is an attitude, a mind set..." Tyler searched for a word, "a Zeitgeist, that's a great old term for it, which, if it runs the course it's on now, will lead to a complete rejection of us. Psy perceivers will be considered absolute aliens, inhuman, something to be feared, controlled, maybe at last, exterminated." Tyler's voice was level, as if she were stating something obvious. "That's the special perception Meryl Acre had. And the problem for me is, now I have it too." Tyler let out a long exhale of breath. "I've had it for a long time. Not with the same kind of clarity Meryl had. But since that night in the park, when she crystallized it for me, I recognize it for what it is. It's the reason I avoid," there was a flicker of sarcasm from Tyler but it was essentially friendly, "what *you* would call civilization." Tyler turned away again and ran the palm of her hand along the fence rail which had long ago been worn smooth. "For years now whenever I've been where there are large concentrations of conventional perceivers, it's as if I'm picking up something, sorting something, which I've never quite been able to make sense out of. It's been like some background sound, a little hum of vibration that's always present. It's hard to describe. It's something that periodically intrudes on my consciousness and reminds me that it's never really gone. It's always left me a little uneasy, a little edgy, but nothing I couldn't live with for the brief times I spent in metro. I ignored it most of the time. I always assumed I was just bothered by not being able to figure out what it was."

Tyler stopped. Without speaking, Dorian prompted. She simply let the words 'and now?' form in her mind.

"And now?" Tyler said. "Now I know what it is and why it makes me uneasy." Her tone continued matter-of-fact and certainty lurked behind her words. "What I know is...Meryl Acre was right. Not about what she did, but about why she did it. Her attempt to act on that awareness, to risk the present in order to save the future."

Dorian tried to respond calmly but her frustration and anxiety were too strong. She burst out, "What you're saying is, because of Meryl Acre's fantasies, you believe you're sorting some perception of, what should I call it? An anti-psy groundswell? Forming everywhere?" The words were challenging, almost contemptuous. "Tyler." Dorian threw out the name like a lifeline. "I shouldn't have to tell you, there can't be such perception, such knowledge. It's impossible. Surely you understand, you're caught in something that was only a projection from Meryl Acre herself, a projection of her own delusions. Something she created in you."

"Another sensible opinion," Tyler said smoothly. "It was mine, once. In fact it's what I told Meryl that night in the park. With even more insistence than is in you now. You can't know any of it, I said. You can't know the future, you can't make knowledge out of uncounted bits of perception." Tyler re-created in herself the same urgency of argument she had felt when she had pleaded with Meryl Acre. Dorian could sort quite clearly the recollected emotions. But it was all remembrance. The present had changed. "But she could, she did," Tyler said with utter conviction and unarguable finality. "And I can too. Meryl Acre wasn't imagining things and she wasn't crazy. And neither am I." Dorian shook her head. "Think about it," Tyler went on. "Think about that knowledge and the horrible dilemma of what to do with it."

Against the rock of Tyler's certainty all argument seemed to break, futilely. "You will grant, I suppose," Dorian said with unusual gentleness, "that you could be wrong."

Tyler's lips curved upward in what should have been a smile, but wasn't. "What, for the sake of argument? Or to show I haven't completely lost my balance? Yes. I'm human. As far as I know. I can be wrong." But her words did not alter her unshakable conviction that she was not wrong. It left Dorian with a deep, wearying sadness.

"All right," Dorian returned, "say, for the sake of argument, you are right. Even at that, surely you don't accept Meryl Acre's solution."

"Kill people? Run the risk of riot in the street today in the hope of saving tomorrow? No, I can't accept any of that." Tyler sorted from Dorian a pervasive sense of relief, surprising in its intensity. She acknowledged the feeling and said, "You didn't think I'd gone that far, did you?"

"No, I guess not."

"I wish I knew where my reaction, or lack of it, falls on the scale of morality. All I know is, it doesn't seem particularly virtuous to me. More like cowardice, or maybe just a failure of nerve."

"Tyler, you don't believe that."

"Well, I'll try to take some satisfaction in the thought you consider I've made the sane choice."

Dorian took Tyler by the shoulder and pulled her around so they faced each other. "A lot saner than becoming the very thing paranoia, the non-psy's paranoia, fears. A lot saner than giving them a legitimate reason to turn against us. A lot saner than Meryl Acre."

Tyler met Dorian's gaze without flinching. "The last in a line of sensible opinions. I have no argument to advance against it. I just have a lot more sympathy with Meryl's situation. It's not an enviable position, sitting as a spectator on the edge of doom because you can think of no action to take which you can consider rational."

There didn't seem to be anything left to say, so Dorian turned to walk back toward the house.

--I know you still think it's all crazy. But it has helped to talk about it. I thank you for that.--

Startled, Dorian stopped in mid-stride. She whirled around and looked back at Tyler in amazement. The impartment had been so swift, so sure, the words had simply flowed into her mind. "That wasn't even hard for you," Dorian exclaimed.

--No. Not hard at all. Not any more.--

"That's incredible." For Dorian the bleak frustration she had felt blew away like clouds in the wind. In its place was fascination and an irrepressible surge of envy. "Since when...?" Her words slid to a halt.

"Since now I suppose, since you're the first person I've tried it with."

"But you knew, didn't you? Since the encounter with Meryl."

"I was pretty sure. I kept remembering how automatic impartment was for me when I used it on Wilkins the night Meryl and Bren were killed."

Dorian's enthusiasm and excitement bubbled up. "Does it feel as natural to you as it seems to?"

"Yeah. It's like something's clicked into place and all the strain is gone."

"And the other things Meryl Acre could do? Impart not just words but emotions, images. Can you do that, too?"

"I don't know. I haven't tried."

"But you think you can, don't you?"

"Maybe. And maybe I'm not ready to find out."

"It would be a shame to suppress an ability like that. Fail to develop it."

Tyler stared at Dorian with dark unfathomable eyes. "Meryl Acre killed eleven people. With that wonderful ability."

Dorian sorted from Tyler a welter of emotions. Anger, frustration, fear all coming together in bitter resentment that for her impartment had been irrevocably tainted. Dorian felt she finally grasped what Tyler was struggling with.

"Tyler, doesn't this explain why you have to believe Meryl Acre was right? To believe her nightmare visions of the future. Believe maybe she had some justification for the killings. So you can live with this, with the legacy she left you. So you don't have to face the reality. That Meryl Acre was a psy with brilliant ability, unheard of ability, ability which somehow she opened for you. But for all that, she was a maniac."

"I'll tell you, Dorian," Tyler said unrelentingly, "it would be easier for me to live with the thought of Meryl Acre's insanity. Easier to do that than to live with the certainty that, however misguided her actions, the knowledge which drove them is real."

Dorian sighed heavily. "And impartment?"

"What about it?"

"What you can do now, how easy it's become for you, that ought to be shared. It's a breakthrough of enormous significance." Tyler's silence was like stone. Uneasily Dorian added, "Anyway, you'll have to tell them, at your next profile review."

"Will I?"

Dorian thought about it. "I guess not. But they won't like it, if they ever find out."

"You don't much like it either," Tyler said. "Although, I grant, for different reasons."

"I'm more than a bit jealous, country mouse. You know that. But this is yours. I won't betray it." Dorian's lips curved into a tight little smile. "Although I might occasionally pester you to change your mind. About sharing, at least with me."

"Maybe. Maybe later." Tyler sorted the disappointment which Dorian did not attempt to repress and said, "I will try to come to terms with all of this. Maybe then," she added without much conviction.

They walked back to the house. The sun was already slanting over the tops of the trees in the line of woods. The house was empty. Rita Fuentes had finished her work and gone home.

Together they walked over to Dorian's ceevee. Dorian, uncomfortable with leaving Tyler to her isolation, searched for some last thing to say. But Tyler spoke first. "Don't worry about it. This," she swept her arm across their line of view, "is what I need. For now, anyway."

For now, Dorian echoed without speaking. Tyler acknowledged it with the slightest tilt of her head. Finally Dorian said, "If there's ever anything I can do. You know. Call me."

Dorian got into her ceevee and started to pull away. She got a last glimpse of Tyler, who stood for a moment and then turned and walked, not into the house, but back along the path that led to the quiet, unpeopled countryside, with its late afternoon yellow green sunlight, and its remote, implacable beauty.

Less than a lifetime later:
Psy Mind: Calculated Risks

—A Free Preview—

Chapter One

The Public Transit car bumped along, keeping its own fitful rhythm. With each of its tremors, Renny Montero could feel her back and legs, clammy with sweat, slide on the worn vinyl seat. As usual, the car's cooling system was no match for the muggy stickiness of the day. It was a familiar discomfort. Renny had years of experience to know that the PT was always too hot in summer, too cold in winter.

But familiarity didn't make it any less irritating, particularly today when her nerves and stomach were dancing to their own erratic cadences. She checked the time. Another five minutes to her stop, about ten minutes to walk up the thruway to Toller Plaza, a couple more minutes to the RanCor building. Once there, the security check would be quick, efficient. After that, up to the HR offices on the fifth floor. And then she needed to be ready, ready to be composed and confident and all the other things necessary to get this job.

Unfortunately, though not unexpectedly, she had had a restless night. She had tossed and turned for too long. And when she had finally dropped off, she had awakened again, wrenched from sleep by a recurring and unpleasant dream. A nightmare in fact, although Renny hated to empower it with that word. She suffered from occasional and, she had been assured by a public sevice medtech, minor bouts of vertigo. But the dream image which cast her into a long dizzying fall always left her deeply unsettled.

At least once she had shaken off the dream's effects, as if her anxieties had been purged, she had slept well the rest of the night. Her dream had not returned to drift into even more frightening images as it all too often did. And she had been able to get an early start. She had planned to have plenty of time to spare once she arrived, to wipe away the grit and perspiration and, with any luck, some of the nervousness.

Renny stared out the grime blurred window. She couldn't resist thinking about what this job would mean, if she could get it. No more Public Transit, no more cubicle-sized apartment, no more Class C comm rating, no more Basic Level energy and consumption allotments.

Keep telling yourself, she thought, there will be other chances. But right now, all Renny hoped was that she wouldn't need any other chances. She had made it through the initial cut in the application process for a corporate job a couple of times before and would have been happy with either of those positions. Happy, hell, she would have been delirious. But to work for RanCor, even to have a chance at that made up for her previous disappointments.

Besides she had often heard you needed to reach the interview stage at least two or three times before you had a realistic chance at a permanent track offer. You didn't need to worry until you got up to five or six tries with still no placement. If that happened, you might as well give up and resign yourself. You had reached the highest level you were ever going to get. Just be glad you weren't stuck in a day laborer's complex, or worse.

Abruptly Renny's train of thought was interrupted. She felt herself bounced forward and then back against her seat. The irregular rhythm of the Public Transit car had broken into a series of even more irregular bumps and then ground to a halt. The general stupor of the passengers around her stirred momentarily into random shiftings of position and barely audible murmurs, all of which subsided quickly. Service interruptions were too common to warrant much reaction.

Renny knew that all too well but she said "Shit" anyway. She said it to herself however. Her lips moved but the word was merely a whisper of air. She craned her neck at the window to see if she could tell where they were. The car seemed to have stopped between station platforms, short of a right-hand bend in the track. Over a retaining wall which followed the curve of the track, she could just make out the far end of the next platform. If she stretched her neck a little more, she could see in the distance the heights of the buildings of Toller Plaza rising in domination above the lower tops of the surrounding buildings.

She checked the time again. As best she could estimate, from where the train had stalled, if she got out and walked, she could make it in time, but under the relentless, midsummer city sun, it would be a hot, dirty walk with little, if any, time left to clean up when she got there. And there was a chance the train could be on its way almost immediately. Then again, it could take two hours.

The grainy sound of the announcement system cut across her thoughts. The long ago recorded voice offered only unreassuring fragments. "...apologize for the inconvenience...short delay...resume service at the earliest..."

Renny's city dwelling instincts told her the delay would be longer than she could afford. Arriving at the interview sweaty and out of breath was still better than arriving late, which would be disastrous.

She levered herself out of her seat, trying not to hit anyone in the head with her carryall and walked along the narrow aisle to the door at the front of the car. She punched the automatic release. A much quieter but far clearer response came from the control panel. "You cannot exit the train at this location." The message was repeated twice more. There were a series of beeps and then silence.

Renny said "shit" again, this time out loud but only the door heard her. She leaned against the wall beside the door and waited. It took almost ten minutes for the car to rumble to life for a few feet before it stopped again.

Renny retried the door and got the same message. After two more jerky starts and stops, the door finally opened at Renny's command. She climbed down from the car. None of the other passengers joined her. Evidently no one else wanted to fight the delay. Or needed to.

She found herself at the end of a walkway leading to the next passenger platform. The walkway was at track level and obviously no longer much used. Renny started walking, stepping carefully over the cracked and buckled concrete. She was busy enough minding her footing not to notice at first the rustle of movement ahead of her.

Suddenly a man appeared at the rounded corner of the retaining wall. He was running, fast and frantically. Renny's head jerked up in surprise and she jumped sideways to avoid him. The man, equally startled, broke stride. One of his feet caught in a break in the concrete and he pitched forward. Arms outstretched, his upper body canted at an acute angle, he took two or three flying steps. For a moment, he looked comical, hanging in the air like an animation character caught in a pratfall. But when he finally lost his balance, there was nothing funny about it. He fell heavily, landing on one of his outstretched arms, and Renny was sure she heard the snap of broken bone. The man cried out in pain and rolled to his side. He clutched his forearm and his hand hung limply, bent at an awkward angle at the wrist.

Before Renny could shake off her surprised immobility, a cluster of people came thundering between the track and the wall in a blur of stamping feet and yelling voices. As they careened toward her, Renny jumped back again.

Someone shoved her and distorted faces pressed in on her. Cries of "psike, psike" shrieked around her. The push of the crowd drove Renny back against the retaining wall. She raised her bag like a shield, but she lost her grip and it clattered to her feet. She gestured frantically toward the train, shouting, "Not me," desperate to make herself heard over the clamor of sound.

She doubted anyone heard her, but it didn't matter. She was outshouted by cries of, "He's the one, that one, over there." The splinter group which had swelled around her swung its attention back to the fallen man and to the larger group which now surrounded him. In the front rank, three or four men with short clubs, their arms rising and falling in a syncopated rhythm, began to pummel the man. He tried to curl into a ball, his good arm raised to shield his head.

The blows fell on him, with dull thunks broken occasionally by sharper clicks when the clubs collided with each other.

The beating continued and the mob pushed in closer. Their feet jostled the man's injured arm and he cried out so loudly that his voice carried over the other sounds. Renny, breathless, frightened, reflexively backed away, but she was stopped by the wall at her back. She could no longer see the man, only the people who swarmed over him, like insects busy at a piece of garbage. The sharp, acid taste of bile rose in her throat and she turned her head away.

But blocking sight only made sound more vivid. Cries of mob rage had settled into determined grunts accompanied by persistent and merciless thudding as blow after blow fell upon its victim.

The beating was as quick as it was vicious. As suddenly as the mob had converged, it dissolved. As if some private signal had been given, the crowd of people separated, most of them running along the track past the stalled train, a couple of them boosting each other over the retaining wall. One of them jostled Renny as he ran past. He kicked her bag a few steps but not deliberately. It was simply in his way.

For a few moments, everything had stopped. No one from the train, and some of them must have noticed the commotion, appeared. There was only Renny and the bloodied, now silent, figure a few feet away, which she didn't want to look at, but couldn't avoid. Later what she remembered seeing was not the psy's battered form but three or four blunt, heavy sticks scattered around him on the ground. Without thinking, her attention still fixed on the injured man, Renny took a couple of labored steps and bent to retrieve her bag. In mid-motion, a handheld amplifier blared at her. "Halt. Enforcement. Don't move."

Half bent over, Renny froze. Two officers approached. One came directly to her, pointed a scanner at her, and then allowed her to straighten up. She stood very still with her arms at her sides.

The other officer advanced toward the man on the ground, who was now motionless. Renny wondered if he was alive. The officer who had come up to her stood directly in front of her. He was a big man and he blocked her view, intentionally she was sure. "Chip or card?" he asked in a flat voice just a step away from rudeness.

"Card," she replied.

"Let's see it."

Renny cautiously withdrew her wallet and slid out the small piece of plastic marked with her optical print. Carefully placing her thumb on the activation sector, she handed it to the officer. He checked it against the scanner results. And then despite the fact he already knew it, he demanded, "Say your name."

"Renata Montero," she answered promptly.

"What are you doing here?" He was still brusque but she noticed the slight relaxation in him as he re-holstered the scanner.

The stalled train was visible farther down the track, so he probably knew the answer to that as well, but Renny furnished it anyway. "I was on the train. I didn't want to wait. I got off to walk."

"What's your hurry?"

Renny took a breath, hoping to calm herself a little. "I'm on my way to a job interview. RanCor at Toller Plaza."

Without shifting his attention away from her, he took out his comm and made a call. She heard him mention her name. He listened to whatever was being said on the other end, made a couple of confirmatory noises, and then disconnected.

She watched him as he considered her. Some subtle change in his posture or expression told her he had satisfied himself. She wasn't an offender. She was just a civilian, a bystander. Turning his head slightly, the officer called to his partner. "What've you got? Psy bashing?"

"Yeah, embed chip reads mid-range 2. He's alive. Head's pretty beat up. Medunit's on its way."

Renny's officer nodded and then asked, "You see what happened?"

Briefly Renny told her story. How she had been walking away from the train and had walked into the mob's pursuit. The officer listened without comment and then handed back her ID card.

"Thank you for your cooperation." His tone had gone from almost rude to perfunctorily polite. "You can be on your way now." He paused. "Unless you need assistance."

"No. I'm OK." It wasn't true, she knew. Her heart was thumping and she felt shaky, but time was pressing on her. Still she needed to ask, "Is this all? Will I be contacted, or something? As a witness, I mean."

"You recognize anybody?"

"No," she said emphatically.

"You know him?" He jerked his head toward the psy.

"No." Her voice rose in pitch. The officer smiled a little, patronizingly. "We appreciate your citizenship. We know where to find you if we need you." His smile turned more genuine, his teeth flashing white against his smooth brown skin. "But I don't think you'll be bothered. These incidents..." He shrugged. "Well, you know, GreatLakes metro covers a lot of ground. These things happen. About all we do is clean up after. Don't get many arrests in cases like this."

He was trying to be nice and she nodded her understanding. "Yeah, I guess not," she said. "Well, then..." Renny knew the officers were finished with her, but it all seemed so unsettled. The sudden violent intrusion breaking the sense of normality and then the equally abrupt return to it.

Renny walked away, part of her still replaying the graphic scene, part of her relieved that it had touched her so little. She checked the time. If she hurried, she would probably just make her interview on time. And if that worked out all right, she might find herself better insulated from the kind of thing she had just witnessed. A little more privilege would go a long way in keeping such unpleasantnesses at a distance.

CPSIA information can be obtained at www.ICGtesting.com
Printed in the USA
242736LV00006B/1/P